ghostoria

Vintage Romantic Tales of Fright

Tam Francis

Plum Creek Publishing
Lockhart

This book is a work of fiction. All of the characters, organizations, and events portrayed in this novel are either products of the author's imagination or are used fictitiously.

GHOSTORIA: VINTAGE ROMANTIC TALES OF FRIGHT

A Plum Creek Publishing Book
P.O. Box 29
Lockhart, TX 78644

ISBN-13: 978-0692264874
ISBN-10: 0692264876

Printed in the United States of America

DEDICATION

To Clara and Chas, thanks for listening.

CONTENTS

1. ROADSIDE PASSENGER

The knock at my window made me jump and drop my cigarette. I didn't know which to attend to first, the cigarette, which might burn a hole in the pink custom upholstery, or the pale figure who loomed at my window. As I bent down to retrieve the cigarette, I hit the automatic window switch with my other hand. Cool night air flooded the car.

I took a long drag of my cigarette, exhaling simultaneously through my mouth and nose, not very lady-like, but it felt good. The figure gave a curt cough and smiled. She had the look of an abused puppy mixed with a drowned rat, dark brown eyes that would look sad even if she were happy, which she clearly wasn't. Her face was tear-streaked and there were red patches around her nose.

"Excuse me, hi, can you help me? I'm lost."

The night had started out completely normal. It had been a little too chilly to have the top down, so I had the window vent open and a fresh breeze blew at my face. I pressed the preset buttons looking for a good song, tired of the same ones over and over. No luck, I caught the middle of Dodie Steven's *Pink Shoelaces*, again, bobbed my head anyway, and checked my lipstick. It had taken me weeks to find a color that matched my car and looked good on me.

I pushed in the cigarette lighter, reached for my pack of Chesterfields and tried to shake one out, but it was stuck. My eyes left the road for a second. When I looked up, what appeared to be a pale figure ran across the middle of the road. I swerved, hit the brakes, and skidded to a halt halfway on the shoulder, and thankfully, not quite into the ditch.

The rearview showed no signs of the specter I'd seen. Sometimes the dark old roads made me a little punchy. I hadn't seen anything but night for miles, then that flutter of light clothing like gossamer wings, and the knock on the window.

Dodie ended her song, I turned down Andy Williams and knew the night was about to get strange.

I took another drag and tried to keep myself from yelling at the figure who seemed to appear out of nowhere at my window.

"You almost made me run my car into a ditch. What were you thinking, and what in God's name were you doing in the middle of the road, in the middle of the night, in the middle of nowhere?"

"I'm sorry, I'm sorry. It's a long story." She hiccupped and stared at me with her dark eyes. Her eyes were the same color as Frank's.

"Okay," I said. "Get in."

"Thank you. You're a lifesaver." She drifted around to the passenger side of the car and began to lift an old dirty suitcase into my car. I almost dropped my cigarette again.

"No!" I yelled, "not in here."

She cringed and looked at me bewildered, then set her bag on the ground. I popped the trunk. It sprung up with a little bounce. I didn't want to get out of the car, but I didn't want her denting my baby or scratching the paint. We met at the trunk and I knocked off as much dirt from her worn case as I could. It looked like a valise my mother would have used, when they used to call them valises. The cavernous trunk held my own bag which I scooted to make room for her brown tweed, so shabby next to my pristine Samsonite.

"This is a real nice car. I especially like the fins. It looks like a rocket. What year is it?" She stroked the pink metal.

"1959. El Dorado. Cadillac, of course."

She continued to run her hand down the slick line of the car which gave me a moment to inspect my roadside passenger. Besides a pale, sad face, her lithe body was draped in an out-of-fashion powder-blue dress, matching wedge shoes and no stockings.

"I bet this car cost a pretty penny," she said as she slid into the seat. "This thing is mint."

"Yes it is," I said with pride and smiled politely.

A disconcerting chill ran up my spine as I pulled out onto the road. I wasn't that old, but she made me feel middle-aged and it was not a feeling I particularly wanted to feel. I turned the radio back up. The Impalas sang, *Sorry (I Ran all the Way Home)*. I hummed to myself, unsure what to say, how to start.

She spoke in a childish airy voice, "Well, I guess you like oldies songs, too. It goes with the car. My name's Emma. What's yours?"

I turned the radio low, but still audible. "Margie," I answered and reached for my pack, shook out another and lit it with the one in my mouth. I flicked the spent butt out the window. She watched as if mesmerized, then opened her mouth to say something, but thought better of it and closed it again. She looked like the goldfish *he* had won for me at the state fair. The Impalas finished their song before I continued.

"Would you like to explain what you were doing out there, by yourself, in the dark?"

She took a deep breath and sighed. Her skin was so pale she appeared translucent, but the warmth of the car had evened her blotchiness and I thought with a little make-up and hair style she could be a very pretty girl. Too bad I didn't have time for it. I always wished I had more time.

She turned her dark eyes to me. I looked away. "My boyfriend and me..." she started to say.

"It's always about a man isn't it?" I nodded knowingly. Frank's face flashed before my eyes and I swerved, cursing myself for letting him into my thoughts. I shouldn't have asked. I should have just taken her down to the roadside diner and not gotten involved, but it was too late and it's what she needed. Maybe we could help each other.

"Well," she continued, "sometimes he gets real crazy mad. I mean, he's well, he's real good looking. And he'll make real pretty babies. And I know he loves me and all. It's just that I didn't want to do it anymore."

"Do what?"

"The activities we were doing, which weren't real nice or very legal, but it wasn't hurting no one." She stopped talking and rung her hands. "Well, it's nothing that bad and don't be thinking like it's that way either, we're both nineteen and all."

"Okay," I said. I could be patient and we had a lot of road ahead of us.

"So, we had stopped at the roadside grave back there, you know, the ones where people leave little white crosses to mark the place where somebody they loved died."

I knew the one she was talking about but kept silent and took another drag, keeping my eyes on the road.

"You wouldn't believe all the funny stuff people leave at the roadside graves: statues, coins, jewelry, clothing, stuffed animals for babies that have died. There's even real nice crosses, not just little wood ones, real nice ones worth some money, means someone really loved them, don't you think?"

I smiled.

"Well, they're not real graves, no one's buried there, but we liked to call 'em roadside graves. Anyway, the point is, we had a big fight and he left me there."

I couldn't hold my tongue. "In the middle of nowhere? In the middle of the night? That doesn't sound like love."

"Well, it wasn't the middle of the night. It was that real pretty time of night when the sun has dropped, but the sky still has a bit of that funny color blue, where the whole world just fades across the heavens."

I closed my eyes for a second and tried to recall the color, but knew I couldn't get it quite right.

"Besides, he was just teaching me a lesson. He'd done it before. I knew he'd come back for me. He said he'd love me forever. He said he'd never leave me."

I looked down my nose and gave her an incredulous look. She ignored me, tucked her hair behind her ear and continued.

"He doesn't really like people telling him he's wrong. He gets all agitated and starts talking about respect and manhood. He was on his own since he was fifteen and he's real tough. I know he'd notta left me if he'd known about the baby. He never woulda done that. But I didn't get the chance to tell him."

"Ah shit," I say out loud. This is too much. What kind of

advice can I give her that will help this mess? "Look, if I had some money I would give it to you. I'm sorry, I can't help you out there."

"I don't need your money. I got plenty of loot. I just need to get ahold of Hank. I know once he hears the blessed news he'll take me back."

"Emma, is it?"

"Yeah."

"Emma, let me tell you something and I want you to listen damn close. Life will not get better. Having a baby will not fix your problems and will not make Frank a better guy."

"Hank."

"What?"

"His name is Hank, not Frank."

"Oh, did I say Frank?"

"Yeah, but you're wrong."'

"I know it seems like it right now, but you have to hear me out. If you have family or money, and you can set yourself up, you have to get away, get away from that man. You have to trust me."

"No I don't." She crossed her arms and stared out the window.

The glass reflected a ghosted image; silent tears ran down her cheeks.

I didn't want to share my story with her. I never liked sharing my story. There must be some other way to convince her.

I reached for another cigarette and opened the window further. She gave a small cough, even though the smoke was drawn through the gap. I didn't know what else to say.

The Drifters sang *There Goes My Baby*. It was too much. I turned the radio off and drove in silence. It was miles before I realized she'd fallen asleep. She looked even younger in sleep. I reached behind the seat and dragged a blanket to the front and fixed it over her with my free hand. It was too small to cover her entire body, but it might give her some comfort.

An hour later she yawned and stretched, then bolted upright. "Oh," she exclaimed and looked at me sheepishly. "I had forgotten where I was. Where'd this blanket come from?"

"The back."

"Thank you, it's very soft."

"Yes."

"If I tell you something will you promise not to turn me in to the cops?"

"I can honestly say I will not turn you in to the cops." It was interesting how a warm car on a dark night could become a confessional.

"We're grave robbers."

"Oh," I said more than a little shocked, but tried not to show it. I wanted to get through to this girl.

"See, that's what he's been doing since he was fifteen. He doesn't know nothing else and he didn't finish school and we made real good money. We hafta keep a move on, though, and always find where new pawn shops are at. You can't believe the stuff people are buried with. But I was saying I wanted to quit it. Get real jobs. But you see, that messed with his male ego. He didn't want to work for someone else, or have someone telling him what to do."

"I understand you love him, but you and your baby need safety. He's not safe."

"I don't want to hear it, lady. I'm grateful for you giving me a ride and all, but I'll be getting my Hank back."

I tried to take another drag of my cigarette, but realized I had smoked it down to the butt. My hands trembled as I scrabbled for the pack and shook out another. I would need fortification for what I was going to say.

"Let me tell you a story," I paused nervous and unsure how to frame my tale.

"I had this friend, a good friend of mine. She had a husband, much like your boyfriend. Only he had a good job and made really good money, and gave her everything she wanted, a nice house, nice clothes, a nice car."

I ran my hand over the curve of the steering wheel and gripped it tightly, coming to the part I didn't like. The cold hard steel steadied my nerves.

"But when he drank he would hit her. And he drank a lot. They had a baby, a beautiful baby girl. She thought he would stop drinking, but he didn't. In fact, he grew worse. She had friends that told her to leave him, her mother told her to leave him, she had choices, but still she stayed. Until one night he was so drunk and beat her so badly she'd had enough. Her cheek was cut, a steady trickle of blood ran down her face, mixing with her tears. Her eye started to swell and the back of her head ached from where he'd banged it against the doorframe."

"Hey, is that something up there? See those lights."

"Oh, yes, are we this far already? That would be Perkly's Diner. It's open twenty-four hours. But I need to finish my story." I hurried on. "So, while he went to the corner mart for another pack of cigarettes and a bottle, she cleaned her face, stuffed a suitcase, wrapped her baby in a blanket and packed them all in her expensive car and drove away."

"Well, that sounds good."

I took another drag on my cigarette and exhaled, slow as I could. "Except she'd been drinking, too. And as she drove, the concussion she didn't know she had, mixed with the alcohol and she passed out." I took another drag.

"Oh, no."

"Oh. Yes."

"I don't want to hear any more."

"She crashed the car into a telephone pole on the side of the road. She and the baby were killed instantly."

"No, no, no. That's not a nice story. I don't like that story. Why did you tell me that story?"

"Because it's true and although I couldn't save her, maybe, if you listen to me, I can save you."

The look of fear on her face gave me hope that my words had sunk in. We heaved silent sobs, but didn't say anything else as I took the turn-off. Yellow diner light spilled across the mostly vacant lot, but I pulled into a dark space at the end. I wasn't ready to lose her to the light yet.

Emma unconsciously dragged the small blanket to her eyes and wiped them dry. I popped the trunk and made my way toward it. As Emma reached for her bag, I put my hand on hers to comfort her. She jerked it away.

"You're so cold," Emma said.

"I know. I'm sorry. Please, please think about what I've said. Please consider making it on your own. Don't go back to Hank. Please."

I slammed the trunk. I wanted to hug her, to keep her safe in my car forever, but knew I couldn't. I sat back in the driver's seat, lit another cigarette and watched her walk toward the diner. Duane Eddy blared *Forty Miles of Bad Road*, again, as I turned the ignition. I was just about to pull out when she came running back.

"I forgot to give you back your blanket."

"Keep it for your baby I don't need it anymore."

I pulled out onto the long road. The night had started out completely normal. It had been a little too chilly to have the top down, so I had the window vent open and a fresh breeze blew at my face. I pressed the preset buttons looking for a good song, tired of the same ones over and over. No luck, I caught the middle of Dodie Steven's *Pink Shoelaces*, again, bobbed my head anyway, and checked my lipstick. It had taken me weeks to find a color that matched my car and looked good on me.

I pushed in the cigarette lighter, reached for my pack of Chesterfields and tried to shake one out, but it was stuck. My eyes left the road for a second. When I looked up, my headlights reflected the pale arm of a hitchhiker with his thumb out. I narrowly missed hitting him, and skidded to a stop, puffing my cigarette while I waited for him to make his way to my car.

2. LONG WAY HOME

The whistle blew long and loud. The two seventeen-year old boys could just make out the chug of the train as it sped their way. Up in a tree, and even as adept as they were, they still wouldn't make it down and across the tracks before the 5:40 Express blocked their path.

They'd have to take the long way home and risk being late. A little old for tree climbing, they held on to their boyish pursuits longer than most kids their age.

Being late might mean a whippin' for Vinnie but it would most certainly be a groundin' for Clayton. One more week until Spring Break and there was no way Clayton wanted to be grounded for the entire glorious week free from tests and teachers, not to mention that the weather was as right as it could be with mosquitoes at a minimum.

Clayton thumped the ground as he swung down from the lowest hanging branch, but the thud was lost in the clacking of the train cars.

"Ahhh hell, we're gonna be late," Clayton yelled to Melvin above the din.

"Well," Vinnie grimaced and yelled back, "we could take the short cut through the cemetery?"

Clayton shuddered at the thought. He wasn't afraid, not in the way most people were. He didn't believe in ghosts, surely if they existed *she* would've tried to contact him. And at one time he thought the trees, the kept grass and monolithic tombstones were beautiful. They'd even played hide and seek there trying to impress the girls, but since his mother died, almost a year ago, he hadn't set foot in the ancient graveyard.

Clayton shook his head *no*, and picked up his bike. "You can go that way, but I'm going the long way home."

"You know I can't be late again or my pop will tan my hide, and you can't be late, or you'll be grounded for all of our Spring Break." Vinnie maneuvered his bike in front of Clayton's. "What am I going to do for a whole week without you and no school? We were gonna go fishin' and we promised to take the girls to the picture show in Seguin."

Clayton knew he was right, but Vinnie didn't understand the ache in Clayton's middle. He was afraid if he saw her grave, or even rode through the graveyard, the hole inside him would get bigger and swallow him up. He didn't know how to explain it to Vinnie, but he also knew Vinnie was right. It was the shortcut or a dismal Spring Break.

Vinnie grabbed Clayton's handlebars and turned him in the direction of the underpass. Clayton squeezed the rubber grips of his bike, his hands already beginning to sweat with the quiet terror building in his gut. He closed his eyes and tried to swallow, but his throat was too dry—he coughed instead. Vinnie handed him his Lone Ranger canteen, really much too old for it, but it served the same purpose as a rabbit's foot for him. Clayton took a deep swig then wiped his mouth on the back of his sleeve, like a warrior going into battle.

"Race ya," Vinnie said and took off down the hill.

Vinnie always gave himself a head start, but Clayton's legs were strong and he'd grown four inches since the start of his junior year. He stood on his pedals and pressed hard. He liked the quick jolt of pain when he pushed his muscles past their natural extent, it made him feel alive. With the incline and hard pumping he caught up to Vinnie. They passed under the shadow of the old bridge at the same time.

Clayton raised up his arms like breaking through a winner's tape. He sat back and cruised for a moment with no hands, no thoughts, just free-floating. As the bike slowed, the front tire began to wobble, and he immediately brought his hands back to the grips and steered toward the path through the cemetery.

His bike bounced over the bumpy lane and a white blur flashed on his left, the direction of his mother's grave. His heart raced. He had a moment of irrational thought that it could be a ghost, her ghost. He was equally terrified and hopeful.

"Hey, hey you? Hi, Hellooo." Vinnie called out from behind him.

"Wha…" Clayton replied, stopped and waited for Vinnie to ride up beside him. "Who me?"

"No dingus, that girl. Did you see where she went?"

"Um, girl?"

"Yeah, the pretty little bird in the white dress?" Vinnie whistled a catcall. "She was something. Not from here, for sure. I would've remembered her."

"Uh, I saw something, but I don't know. I thought maybe…"

"You'd seen a ghost," Vinnie said, laughed, and then punched Clayton in the arm. "Let's see if we can find her."

Clayton didn't want to go that close to his mother's grave, but another part of him wanted to confirm what Vinnie saw, just to make sure it was a real girl. Vinnie started to pedal his bike across the graves. Clayton grabbed his arm.

"We should walk the bikes and stick to the bottom of the graves."

"What do you mean?"

"I mean, don't walk on the dead, it's not respectful. Try to keep toward the space between where their feet might be and where the next headstone is."

"Yeah, right. Uh, sorry Clay. You know I can be a dink sometimes." The rhythmic clack of the 5:40 Express train filled the awkward silence.

Clayton quelled the churning feelings and shrugged to hide the involuntary shudder that rippled through his body. They didn't have time for this, he thought.

"Three minutes. I'll give you three minutes." He made a face at Vinnie. "Let's go quail hunting."

"That's the spirit," Vinnie said and then smacked himself in the head. "Uh, I mean…"

Clayton playfully socked Vinnie in the shoulder. "Shut up, dingus."

"Boo!" said the girl in the white dress as she jumped out from behind a large tree trunk headstone.

Clayton and Vinnie jumped out of their skins and almost dropped their bikes. Clayton recovered first and immediately understood what Vinnie was talking about. The girl, or rather young woman, clinging to the concrete *Woodmen of the World* gravestone, looked like an angel sent to earth.

Her skin glowed clear and snowy, her eyes green like a cat's. The white dress, although not too tight, fit snuggly around her full breasts and curvy hips, pale shapely legs extended from the skirt's edge. The rush of heat he'd been unable to control every time he looked at cute girls, tripled, and sent a shot through his body. He had a strong desire to grab her and kiss her like a leading man in the movies.

"Hi, I'm Clayton, this here's Vinnie."

She giggled and flitted behind the trunk, peeking out from the other side. "I'm Lily."

"So, um, come here often?" Vinnie asked.

Clayton looked at him and shook his head, a smirk played across his mouth.

"No, this is my first time here. My father is the new caretaker. We're just moving in," she answered with no hint of recrimination to Vinnie's awkward come-on line.

"Into what? The cemetery?" Vinnie said.

Her brow furrowed. The wind blew her dress exposing her creamy thighs. Both Clayton and Vinnie's eyes flicked to her legs before she smoothed down her dress. She appeared to be unaware of their gawking.

"Well, yes," she paused, "and no. We're moving into the old gatehouse on the far side." She pointed to the oldest part of the cemetery.

"Well, we have to go that way on our way home. Would you like a lift?" Clayton asked and gestured to his handlebars.

"Sure."

"Walk back with us to the pathway and I'll give you a ride." He turned his bike.

Vinnie also turned his bike but with much stomping, cranking of his handlebars, and muttering, "I saw her first."

When they reached the path, Clayton showed her where

she could put her hands and feet to hoist herself onto the handlebars. He held the bike steady as she climbed up—that was always the hardest part. Once he got a few pedals in, the bike would miraculously straighten itself out. It had something to do with physics and motion, but he couldn't remember the exact theory. Her hands, cold from gripping the concrete headstone, brushed his and sent a tingling through his body. He wanted to hold her hands in his and warm them, but he kept his grip firmly in place. He wouldn't impress her by spilling her off his bike.

The train whistled once more, which meant it was halfway through the town. They had seven more minutes before they had to hightail it to be home on time.

"We've gotta hit the bricks and make like a kite," Vinnie said.

"I know," Clayton replied.

"What bricks? There aren't any bricks here and I don't see a kite," Lily said.

"Yeah, uh, you know, get a move on, hustle, fly like a kite? Where'd you move from anyway, Siberia?"

"Can it, Vinnie," Clayton said.

"Yeah, yeah."

"Well here we are Miss Lily. Will we see you in school tomorrow?" Clayton asked.

"Oh, uh, well I..."

"Don't be a dink, Clay. Her old man ain't gonna sign her up till *after* Spring Break."

"Yes, that's it. Yes," she replied.

"I'm the smart one," Vinnie said and bowed to her.

She smiled and hopped off the handlebars. Her hand brushed Clayton's again and the skirt of her dress swished around her legs in a way that made Clayton uncomfortable and amazingly happy at the same time.

"See you tomorrow," she said and skipped toward the old shack.

Clayton couldn't remember how many years it had been since the cemetery had a caretaker living in the small quarters. The place would take a lot of work. He had a hard time reconciling the old shack with her pristine appearance. It was only after she disappeared behind the old place that Clayton felt the return of the vacuum inside him, though it was a little less than before.

"Race you," Vinnie said, already three lengths away from Clayton.

❉ ❉ ❉

Much to Vinnie's displeasure and slight jealousy, Clayton had seen Lily every day after school. At the end of the week Clayton found himself on top of a blanket, on top of Lily, under a tree in the cemetery. He pressed his body into hers and nibbled her neck. She giggled and pulled his weight tighter to her wriggling body. Clayton slid his mouth back to her lips. She kissed him voraciously, sending fire through his body.

He knew he should slow down, he felt a slight disrespect to the dead, and when he voiced this concern to Lily earlier in the week, she dismissed his worry and guided his hand to her plummy breasts. He knew about easy girls, but he didn't care. She was beautiful and sweet and closed the hole in his heart.

Although they were well hidden between an old elm and a large obelisk, the crack of a twig startled Clayton enough to roll off of Lily and sit up. With obvious frustration she sat up too and smoothed her skirt, but kept it fanned at mid-thigh.

"Oh, it's just *that* man," Lily said. "He comes every morning. He's off his schedule today, he's late. Isn't it sweet though, to love someone so much, even after death? It would be wonderful to be loved forever and ever."

From Clayton's vantage point he watched the solitary man walk across the graveyard. A bouquet of flowers hung from the mourner's hand. He knew the man and knew where he was walking. He didn't know why, but he kept the information to himself. Nor would he let on to his father when he saw him later at dinner.

"Lily. Lily. I know you're out here," a gruff voice called from the opposite direction.

"Oh, no, that's my father. I'd better go," Lily said.

Clayton looked in the direction of where her old man shuffled through the graves. *He looked old enough to be her grandfather, not her father.* He glanced once to see his own father put the flowers on his mom's grave.

Lily bent down and gave Clayton a warm kiss on the mouth. His passion stirred again. He rose to his knees and tried to embrace her, but she slipped away leaving him wanting.

He watched as she spirited away from him to the old man, who scooped her up like a child, carrying her with two arms. She returned the gesture with flailing, childish movements. Then she whispered something in his ear and he set her down. They walked away with Lily's arms entwined in her father's, her head resting on his shoulder. An irrational stab of jealousy shot through Clayton.

He turned his attention to his father at his mother's grave. A trick of the light made it look like there was a faint glow around his father. It quickly disappeared with the rolling clouds.

Clayton waited until his father had gone before clearing up the blanket. He replayed his last trigonometry test questions so he wouldn't think about Lily and how good her body had felt against his and how much more he wanted to do with her. He pulled his bike from behind the small mausoleum and rode home for an early dinner before meeting Vinnie and the gang.

He and his father ate in silence. Clayton wanted to reach out to his father, but didn't know what kind of gesture would make sense, and he certainly didn't want to talk about seeing him at his mother's grave.

It was his father who spoke first. "Eat up your green beans son, you're looking a little tired." He stood and began to clear his plate and glass, then set them down and clapped Clayton on the back.

He reached up and patted his father's hand. "Yes, Pop." The moment passed. His father picked up his dishes and trudged to the kitchen.

Clayton ate his green beans and drank all his milk. Now that his father had mentioned it, he was feeling a little tired after all. He thought maybe he'd stay home. He'd ring Vinnie and tell him, but just as he had that thought, the toot of Vinnie's brother's hotrod honked from the street. He cleaned up his dishes and jogged out the front door. Spring Break had begun.

He couldn't stop thinking about Lily and how much more fun it would be if she could come, but she'd said her father was very strict and she wasn't allowed to date. He ran through the trigonometry questions, again.

Clayton and Vinnie started out their week of freedom by heading off to the Dixie Drive-In movies in Seguin. It was a double feature: *Lady and the Tramp* and *Rebel Without a Cause.* Clayton was so tired he dozed in the Model A roadster, but was jolted awake as the rebuilt '29 bounced over the sloped landscape and settled in the sea of parked cars, tilted on frozen waves.

Vinnie's brother, Gil, cranked up the radio when *Dance with Me Henry* came on. Everyone jumped out and started jitterbugging around the car.

"Come on Clay," Susie called and pulled him out for a dance.

Although he was tired, he loved the Georgia Gibbs song and loved to dance even more. He led her down the small hill to the flat lane between the inclines. It was dustier, but easier than dancing on the slope. The teens who weren't sneaking a smoke or making a run to the concession stand, were already kicking up dust clouds and twirling around. Clay spun Susie through intricate turns and tucks, always on beat. The strange pall that had clung to him since seeing his father at the cemetery gradually melted away in the fine spring evening.

After the Gibbs song the Platters slowed it down with *Only You*, but Clayton was in no mood to slow dance.

"Well," Clayton coughed and fanned the dusty air, "would you like to go get a quencher?"

"Sure, that would be swell. Let me get my pocketbook."

"Nothing doing, Suze, I got it, don't worry about it. Whaddaya want?"

"Grape Nehi if they got 'em."

They walked toward the concession building. Clayton turned to sneeze and had just enough time to pull his hankie out of his pocket.

"Oh, no Clay, you've got a bloody nose," Susie said. "Look."

Clayton saw the bright red blot staining the white hankie. "Oh, that's weird."

"It musta been all the dust. Come over and sit down." She guided him to one of the picnic tables in the playground area. "Pinch your nose."

"I thought I was supposed to lean my head back," he said.

"No, that's all wrong. My mom's the grade school nurse you know, and she says you don't want to get too much blood in your stomach, or it can make you vomit." She squinted at him. "Do you feel like you're going to vomit?"

"No," he replied, but thought, *I wish you'd stop saying vomit, this is embarrassing enough.*

"Well, let me get you some ice. That can help, too."

"No, I'm all right. Look, I think it's stopped now." He took the hankie away from his nose. "See."

"Well, if you're sure. But you just wait right here, I'll get our soda pops."

"Uh, okay." He did feel a little dizzy. He dug in his pocket and pulled out three quarters. "Will you grab me an Abba Zaba bar and get whatever else you want."

"How 'bout some popcorn?"

"Sure," he replied. As he watched her walk into the busy building he had the oddest thought: *I should've saved my energy for Lily and stayed home.*

❀ ❀ ❀

Spring Break flew by with some fishing in the creek, some dancing at the malt shop, some lazing around, and a lot of necking with Lily. Clayton was so hot and bothered he'd taken cold showers every morning and every evening when he'd come home from meeting Lily at the graveyard. He'd even jumped into the creek where he and Vinnie were fishing that afternoon. He couldn't stop thinking about her and felt like he had a fire burning inside him that only she could put out.

Even though Clayton thought Lily's plan was a little creepy and weird, he went along with everything she said. He'd even gone to Vinnie's brother and, after much hemming and hawing, asked him if he had any rubbers. Gil had clapped him on the back and dug in his wallet and handed over the smart man's protection, but not before he gave Clayton some good-natured ribbing and threatened to tell Vinnie.

Why Clayton didn't want Vinnie to know, he couldn't say. He still wasn't sure he'd know the right time to use the thing and hoped the opportune moment wouldn't prove too awkward.

He lay in his dark room and watched the clock tick off minutes, the glow-in-the-dark hands crawled to the hour. He thought of taking another cold shower, but didn't want to wake his father. It would be harder to sneak out if he was awake. Instead, he turned his mind back to his math sums.

Nothing he tried would take his mind from Lily, her creamy skin, soft breasts and warm body. He hoped he wouldn't have another bloody nose. He'd had two more since the one at the drive-in and thought maybe he was getting some kind of spring cold or had developed allergies. That did it—he thought about blood running out his nose while he was trying to kiss Lily. It momentarily settled his excitement, until he pictured Lily holding his handkerchief to his nose, and then holding his head to her breasts, his mouth inches from her nipple.

It was only ten o'clock. He was supposed to wait until eleven, but couldn't stand it another minute. He had to be with her. The knapsack with the candles, matches, blanket and cooking sherry were packed and ready. It was strange to put his hand on the bottle of cooking sherry his mother had touched, left over from another life, a fuller life.

His mother had been a wonderful cook, but no matter how hard he tried, he couldn't remember how her Beef Stroganoff tasted. He could almost hear the sizzle and recall the smell of the cooking sherry as she'd poured it over the mushrooms and sliced meat. His chest tightened and his eyes stung. He shifted his thoughts to Lily and wondered where she thought he could find wine. The cooking sherry would have to do.

He slung the knapsack over his shoulder and held his Chucks in his hand as he crept down the hall. The screen door squeaked, but Clayton made sure not to let it snap back. He strapped the pack to the back rack of his J.C. Higgins and headed toward the cemetery, no longer discomfited by the proximity of his mother's grave, a gift Lily's presence had given him. He'd even taken to stopping by his mother's gravesite before his Lily rendezvous. Tonight though, he thought he'd skip the visit.

The night was bright which made the streamline headlamp on his bike superfluous, but he switched it on anyway. Tree leaves danced in the soft breeze and the night clung to winter's chill, not ready to give into the longer days. The full moon held court turning the night into monochrome shades of gray. *Woodmen of the World* headstones looked as real as the elms and oaks that surrounded them. Clayton rolled passed the graves and trees, parking his bike behind the largest of the family crypts. He switched off his headlamp, untied his pack in the dark of the moon shade and made his way to the crypt doors.

He didn't know why, it made sense, but was surprised to find them locked. He'd have to wait an excruciating forty-five minutes for her to arrive. His desire trumped his nervous fears and he could hardly wait to see Lily.

He decided to visit his mother's grave after all, hoping it would distract him and kill time. He wished he had something to take to her, to leave at her grave, like his father had. Lily wouldn't miss one of the nine candles, but it would be too much of a fire hazard and too much like a solitary eye spying on his monkey business in the cemetery. He chose instead the sherry and would pour his mother a toast of love and remembrance. Yes, that seemed all right, he thought.

As he was returning from his mother's grave he saw the unmistakable blur of radiance. His heart sped up and a flush swept across his body. His strides grew longer and noisier. She looked up from her place at the crypt door and skipped across the distance. Clayton took her in his arms and crushed her body to his.

His mouth found hers and he devoured her soft lips. She tasted of honey and cool creek water. He ran his hands down her back scooping her buttocks pulling her tighter to his middle. He didn't want to rush it but desire consumed him.

He drove his body into hers not realizing she had been walking backwards until she stiffened against the door of the crypt. He pressed her into the cold marble, running his hands down her front, unbuttoning the tiny buttons on her dress front. The moonlight transformed her white dress into silver and her creamy skin into pale gray satin.

"Not out here," she whispered, wriggled out from under him and turned the door handle. Clayton had to reel back, sweeping her with him to keep from falling over as the door swung inward. He caught his balance by swinging her around in a dance move. She giggled and ducked under his arm.

"Did you bring everything?" she asked.

"Yes, it's on the doorstep."

"Well then."

"Right." Clayton grabbed the pack. When Lily came over to inspect, he pulled her tight and stole another kiss. She kissed him back but it was more perfunctory than passionate. Her hands were already pulling out the bag's contents.

"Oh Lily, you're driving me crazy. I think I love you, you know."

"I know," she said and giggled again.

Clayton thought sometimes she seemed childlike and innocent and other times worldly and womanly. Even with the giggle, tonight, she seemed self-possessed and womanly.

She went to work setting out the candles in even intervals. Clayton trailed her, nipping kisses whenever he could. She always acquiesced and even allowed him to lean her against the tomb walls letting him work himself into a lather before gently pushing him away or ducking under his arm. Clayton marveled at the silhouette of her body in the candlelight. He could see every delicious curve and could barely wait to touch it. *She is beautiful, and I will have her tonight.*

She laid the blanket in the middle of the candles and gestured for Clayton to join her in the center.

Clayton was unsure if he should undress, but liked the idea of her undressing him, and him undressing her. He would not rush it even though every fiber of his body wanted to. He would follow her lead.

She pulled the bottle of sherry out of the pack. "What is this?"

"Um, well, it's cooking sherry?"

She looked bewildered like she had never heard of cooking sherry before. She unscrewed the cap and smelled it.

"It will do. Take a sip and hold the liquid in your mouth. I will take a sip and when I take the bottle away, kiss me, letting the liquid mingle."

He did as she told. The sherry nipped sweet and bitter at the same time, though when it met her mouth and their tongues twined, it mellowed and tasted like caramel. He moved to lay her down, but she pulled away.

"Not yet. Have another sip and take my breast."

She opened her dress and slid the top off, letting it rest on her hips. Then, she unbuttoned his shirt, tossed it to the corner and tugged his tee-shirt over his head. It too, went toward the corner, not quite making it that far. Clayton took another sip of sherry, Lily arched her back, candlelight dallied on her skin. Clayton leaned down...

The crypt door burst open extinguishing the candlelight, but the moon glow was enough to reveal the scene. Lily quickly pulled her dress over her exposed breasts. Clayton reached for his shirt, shoving it over his head.

"I knew you were up to something," her father roared.

"How...how are you awake?" she asked.

"I didn't eat the food you prepared, I kept it in my mouth long enough to spit it out when you weren't looking. Some of it got into me, but not enough to keep me asleep all night."

"Oh, I see," she said.

"You will not have him," her father roared and pointed his finger at Clayton.

"Excuse me sir, I know how this looks, but I assure you, I love your daughter and she loves me," Clayton said.

Her father shook with laughter, clutching his gut. The corner of his mouth drew up to one side into an ugly sneer.

"I am not her *father*. Is that what she told you?" He laughed again and sputtered into a hacking cough.

Clayton didn't know what to think but knew he had to get Lily away from this man. The man must be holding her against her will, or must have kidnapped her, or some other explanation. Clayton couldn't think straight and didn't want to think about why she seemed young and old at the same time. He had to get her away. He would take her to his house. His father would understand.

Clayton grabbed the bottle of sherry and cracked it against the wall. It wasn't like in the movies. It took several knocks before the glass shattered. And it was messier. Sherry splattered over his pants and shirt, but he held the bottle at the man like a weapon.

"I don't want to hurt you, but I will if I have to. Lily, get behind me."

"Your bravado would be comical if it weren't so earnest," said the old man as he shook his head.

"No, don't hurt him." Lily grabbed the bottle from Clayton.

"See there, what'd I tell ya. She still needs me." The old man looked Clayton up and down. "She must not have had you yet or she wouldn't need me. Looks like I got here just in time."

From the back wall of the crypt a bright light rushed toward Lily. As it reached her it became a solid figure of a woman. The glowing lady threw her weight into Lily and enveloped her, knocking her forward. Lily stumbled toward the old man and tried to change direction, but the woman had her hand on Lily's wrist, the jagged edge jutted forward and the bottle sliced clean through his jugular. Blood spurted over Lily drenching her white dress in bright red.

The man clutched at his neck and crumpled to the ground. "I'll love you forever, Lily," he gurgled with his last breath.

The shriek of a thousand angry crows rose up from where Lily stood. "Noooooo."

Like a shell of ash, every bit of her skin, hair and clothing turned dark gray, then black, exploding for a moment before condensing and imploding to nothing.

Clayton felt as if a large weight had been lifted from his body, then replaced with an empty void, a deep loss and sorrow he could barely stand. He stumbled to the steps of the crypt. His body folded and sunk to the top stair. He shook with deep, heaving sobs. A light cool sensation touched his shoulder and enveloped him in a cloud of light and love. His mother cradled his head and patted his back. It took a long time before he spent all of his tears and finally dragged his sleeve across his wet face.

"Are you real?" he asked.

"Only as real as Lily was, and only until the sun rises."

"But how? I don't understand? Why have you never come before?" He ran his fingers through his hair. "I wished for it, I prayed for it."

"I cannot answer all your questions because I do not know all the answers. In some ways I am no better than Lily."

Clayton gave her a confused look.

"That poor man..."

"Oh my god, he's dead, she killed him. You killed him? I killed him? " He looked behind him and found the crypt empty.

"Whaa..."

"She *killed* him a long time ago. I just released him from his prison on earth. He would not have lived long without her."

"Mother, you're talking in riddles."

"I'm sorry. I'm not used to organized, focused thought. The man you thought was her father was only thirty-nine. He met her when he was fifteen."

"I still don't understand."

"What she did to him, sucking the life from him, so that she could live, was what she intended to do to you. I couldn't let that happen. When you began to visit me at my grave my energy and thoughts coalesced and I was able to see beyond my limits. I knew I had to protect you."

Clayton wanted to protect her. He and his father were supposed to protect her, save her, but they failed. He squeezed her tighter. She continued explaining.

"I saw her for what she was and I could not let her have my baby boy. Though, look at you, you're almost a man."

She brushed a lock of hair from his forehead.

"Your father's love allowed me the power to manifest, but at a cost. His life with be shortened by months."

Clayton wiped more tears from his eyes. Worry, confusion, anger, fear, remorse, abandonment, love and hope swirled inside him. "I was in love with a ghost? I thought she loved me. "

"That was not love." She embraced her son. "I'm so sorry I left such a hole in your heart. Know that I will always love you. Be kind to your father, the hole in his heart is even bigger than yours."

"Don't go," Clayton said. He tried to embrace her, hold her to the earth, but she faded away. His hand that held her, turned empty in the heavy air.

He sat for a long time without moving, shedding a few more tears before he finally gathered the blankets and candles into his pack and secured it to his bicycle. He shoved one candle and the matchbook into his pocket and walked to his mother's grave. The candle wax dripped like tears when he melted the bottom to affix it to the top of her headstone.

He lit the candle.

Got on his bike.

And knew he would never take the long way home again.

3. RECEPTION

oarfrost covered the ground, but it was warm enough that my breath made no cloud. I pulled my wool coat tight anyway; the fur collar tickled my chin. The office door clicked in the silent morning, and I was surprised to be the first to arrive. A flash of light or movement caught my eye and startled me, but I was tired and hadn't had any coffee yet.

I hung my jacket on the coatrack and draped my beaded sweater on the back of my chair, unneeded. My phone sat silent at the desk, it usually started ringing the moment I walked in the door. I was pleased to have time to catch up on unfinished work and grab a cup of joe.

I filled the percolator with water and coffee and checked my inbox bin. Nothing new. I took out the unfinished correspondence, inserted it into my trusty Underwood, and turned the knob. The clacking keys echoed like running footfalls in the quiet office and the sound gave me a chill. I couldn't shake the eerie feeling that I had done this before and been here alone before.

"Verna."

I jumped out of my seat.

"Yes, hello?" I looked around, but didn't see anyone, and decided to chalk it up to a car horn or music from an open window. City noises often sounded like conversation.

The smell of coffee filled the empty office. I poured myself a cup and went back to work. After an hour had passed with no boss and no coworkers, I began to think everyone had taken a snow day or an ice day, or it was a Monday holiday I'd forgotten.

"Verna," said a faraway voice.

"Hello, is someone there?"

I was sure I heard something this time, and it wasn't traffic sounds or the percolator. I took my coffee cup, like a meager shield or a familiar friend, and went searching for the mysterious voice. As I passed by the boardroom I heard what sounded like laughter behind the doors. The boss had a reputation and I wasn't sure if I should open the doors. Perhaps he'd given everyone the day off and forgotten to tell me?

I knocked and waited.

No answer.

The pocket doors hissed at me as they slid open to reveal

an empty office. It was a relief, but a bit disconcerting. I knew I'd heard a voice. I slammed the doors shut in frustration.

"Verna."

The voice sound again, this time from the hall. I turned and caught a figure rounding the corner, but when I began to run after it, my coffee spilled, splashing over the linoleum and my favorite platform pumps. The coffee beaded and ran in little rivers off my freshly polished shoes.

My anger flared. Someone was teasing me and I didn't like it. I should've clean up the coffee mess right away, but I wanted to follow the sound. I made another lap around the office. Nothing.

I tried to forget about the voice and did forget about the spilled coffee and went back to work. My fingers shook as I banged at the Underwood. It seemed to help to pound at the keys, each fingertip a little hammer.

Not long into my third assignment a loud sound crashed down the hall. I jumped up and sprinted toward the noise. My shoe hit the coffee slick, my ankle twisted and my foot slid out from under me. I hit the floor after a series of comical contortions and wasn't sure if I should laugh or cry, but was grateful no one was in the office to witness my inelegance.

"I'm so sorry, I didn't mean to make you fall. Let me help you up."

A shimmering woman in a flowing dress stood before me and offered me her hand. I closed my eyes and muttered under my breath. "Not real, not real, not real." Fear washed over me in alternating waves of nausea and excitement.

No one had ever said anything about the office building being haunted, but it was old and I couldn't explain the figure in front of me. Could it be a spirit? I opened one eye to see if she was still there. She was. A violent shudder ran through my body.

"Please, I need your help," she said.

I opened both eyes. The figure appeared to be floating, but her dainty feet rested on the linoleum. She had a sweet, sympathetic smile and with her hand stretched toward me it felt rude not to take it, even if she was a ghost.

When I clasped her hand, it was solid enough, and her wispy frame belied her strength. She pulled me easily to my feet in one graceful movement.

"Hello, Verna, I'm Sera."

"Are you a ghost?"

"More or less. Can you please help me?" she asked again.

"What can I do to help you?"

"Follow me."

I followed her down the hall to the double doors of the boardroom. They stood firm and closed as I had left them. I knew the room to be vacant and wondered why she would bring me to an empty office.

She slid open the large wooden doors and tucked them into their wall pockets. I staggered a few steps back, but she held her arm at my waist and kept me from falling or running away, which was my first inclination.

Seated around the carved mahogany table sat different versions of me, from important times in my life. I shook my head in disbelief. For the second time that day I didn't know if I should laugh or cry. I didn't understand what I was seeing. She laid a soft hand on my arm.

"Verna dear, I'm sorry but you died last night."

I turned to run. She wouldn't let me. I tried to slip through her arms and slide to the floor. If I could just lay down and wake up. She wouldn't let me.

"Verna."

"No. That's not possible. I'm not sick. I'm too young. No!" My eyes filled with tears, but when I looked into her eyes, I was calmed and able to ask a question I wasn't sure I wanted an answer to. "How?"

"You had an aneurism in your sleep. You went very peacefully," she answered.

"No. No. No."

It couldn't be. I wouldn't accept it. I broke free and ran down the hall to the exit. I pulled the door open and found myself not walking outside, but into the office again, like some awful Salvador Dali painting. I beat the door with my fists.

"No."

My body sagged against the door. I slid down to the floor, my legs splayed in front of me like a schoolgirl in a sandbox, my face in my hands. I sat this way for who knows how long. Two seconds? An hour? A day? An eternity?

Sera returned and beckoned me up, her arms outstretched. She took both my hands in hers and again pulled me to my feet.

"Verna, please help me." She led and I followed her back to the boardroom, my sense of time, of self, of feeling seemed to drain away with each step. "You must choose," she said when we arrived.

"Choose?"

"You get to repeat one perfect day for your afterlife, which do you choose?"

It was like looking into a carnival mirror, only my face wasn't distorted in size and shape, but in time. I pointed to my youngest me.

"Look at me there, at five-years-old in pig-tails and pressed dress, ready for my first day of school. I spent two weeks picking out that dress and choosing the hair ribbons."

I instantly thought of Miss Hellums and hadn't in years. Her kindness had stayed with me all of my school days. But that first day, I'd been so scared and unsure. Miss Hellums helped when Nancy Coodigan pulled out my ribbons, threw them in the mud, unraveled my braids, and called me Verna Worma. I'd hidden behind the groundskeeper's shed and vowed never to return to school.

Miss Hellums found me fumbling the knots in my hair, tears thick on my dark lashes. She pulled a brush from her pocket and handed me a kerchief with an embroidered violet at the corner. She said I could keep it. I still have it. She brushed my hair and re-braided it. Then she took the ribbon from her hair, cut it in half and tied it at the end of my braids.

"That wasn't a perfect day though," I said.

"But look at how the five-year-old you is smiling."

"No. Not that day. Maybe, me at seven?"

My puppy, Maisie, sat in my lap, her head resting in the crook of my elbow. I'd forgotten how tiny she'd been with her floppy ears, and fluffy black fur, a red bow around her neck. The moment I laid eyes on her I was in love, and she was in love with me. I knew, even at seven, we had to protect each other and take care of each other.

I'd seen pictures of Bette Davis holding her Scottie dog in Modern Screen magazine, and I had to have one just like Ms. Davis. Mama had given me Maisie for my seventh birthday.

"A little girl and her dog, what could be happier?"

My gut stabbed with the pain of a fresher memory: the day I came home from Secretarial School and Mama said Maisie was gone. At first I was sure she'd meant Maisie had run away, but my Maisie never ran away, she was a perfect lady.

She had died without me. Alone. Why hadn't she waited for me? Why hadn't she hung on so I could have seen her through and held her paw?

The pain in my heart flared brighter than all my previous pains. Worse than Gil dumping me before prom, worse than the news that Uncle Phil had died of dysentery in India, worse than my boyfriend Roy enlisting and leaving on a train to join the war.

"No, not that one, my memory of my Maisie is laced with too much pain."

"But Maisie lived a long and happy life," she replied.

"It is still too painful."

My ghost guide grimaced and nodded her head in understanding. I looked to the next me.

Gawky, but cocksure ten-year-old me, a new smile of confidence, self-worth and accomplishment from swimming out to the platform in the middle of the lake. Every year we would take our family vacation camping and fishing at Evergreen Lake in Ohio. For four years I'd tried, without success, to reach the platform where the older kids hung out, and that summer, I'd done it.

I dove into the spring-fed water and drove my young body, pushing passed the pain and through the cramps building in my side. I still wasn't invited to hang out with the teens, and no one asked me to dance at the camp hoedown, but I'd achieved a goal and knew each summer would get better, and one day I would be part of the gang.

"Good, no sadness there."

"No, but swimming for eternity sounds exhausting." I tried to laugh, but it came out thin and artificial, which it was. I didn't want to choose.

"Keep going," she prodded. "That one looks good."

She pointed to the version of me on my first day of high school in a new city, in a new state. I had deliberated for weeks on what to wear the first day and settled on a green gabardine skirt with three rows of rick-rack trim and my gray, green, and white striped blouse with matching bolero jacket and new t-strap shoes.

A group of girls looked at me, whispered something, and laughed, but then a miracle happened. The cutest boy I ever saw walked by and told me he liked my style, asked me if I was new, and offered to walk me to class. After that the girls were nicer and invited me into their group. I had friends and a boyfriend. Gil and I went steady until our senior year but he threw me over for an able-grable, the kind of girl I wasn't going to be for him. He dropped me right before prom.

I shook my head *no* to that day, too.

"Well, how about this last one?"

It was me at eighteen, only two years ago, but I looked so much younger. It was the day I fell in love with Roy. Bob Wills and his Texas Playboys played at a big band dance. Roy strolled in with a pack of new cadets and when I laid eyes on him, my whole body lit up. I felt alive for the first time since Gil.

We'd spent every moment of his two week liberty together. We necked in the park, and it was so much more exciting than the attention I'd received from Gil. My head swirled and my toes curled.

We canoodled in the movie theater, and burned up the leather on the dance floor. He danced the jitterbug like a Hollywood hoofer and waltzed like Fred Astaire.

I gave him my picture and my heart to bring back when

the war was over, but the war wasn't over.

"I don't want to choose, I can't choose. Every happy day is complicated with extra bits, extra memories, no day is completely happy."

"You won't remember the future you, you'll only remember what you know up to that age. Does that help?"

"No. It's too much to ask of someone. How can one day be more perfect than any other? How can one day be worth living more than the others? It's the sum of our days, the contrast that make our lives...No, no, no! This isn't fair." I turned away from my other selves. "What happens if I don't choose?"

Sera shook her head and looked at me in sympathy, "Then we will repeat this day until you choose. You will continue to come into an empty office, meet me, and see your other selves. Choose. Please."

"Have we done this before?"

"I cannot answer that," she said, but something in her compassionate eyes made me think we had.

"But I barely got to live. It's not fair."

"There are some who have lived even less than you."

"But I'll never marry. I'll never know a man. Roy." I whispered, "I'll never have his babies, or have grandchildren, or own a house with a picket fence."

I ran from the room to my familiar desk chair. My sweater hung limp, the sparkling beads and pearls like accusing eyes. I was cold, but I wasn't, but wanted my sweater on my body. I fumbled for it and couldn't feel it. I reached for my coffee mug, but my fingers couldn't grasp the ceramic handle. I tried typing, but my fingers were unable to press any keys. I looked down at my hands and could see through them.

Sera came to my side and held my hand. I felt the dichotomous warmth and coolness of her glowing skin. My hand did not pass through hers. She held me while I cried, until I had no more tears and finally handed me a handkerchief with an embroidered violet. Then she gently guided me back to the boardroom.

"Please choose."

"Can I choose to be like you?" I asked.

"No, I'm not so much a spirit like you; I'm a Seraph, one of the Seraphim Celestial Beings."

"Like an angel?"

"More or less. Now dearest, please choose."

A last tear rolled down my cheek. "I choose none of those days."

She hung her head in an expression of infinite pity and patience.

"I choose an ordinary day," I said. "A day where the sun is shining and there are no chores and no school. A day where I lay under the shade of a large Elm and read Elizabeth Barrett Browning to Maisie, the clean smell of grass tickling my nose. A day where I tell my mother I love her, before I've noticed she's getting old. A plain day where I eat a sensible meal of toast with blueberry jam, the berries hand-picked from our backyard. For lunch a BLT on rye and maybe green beans and mashed potatoes for supper. An ordinary day where nothing special happens, but it will be the most extraordinary day, because it will be a day like any other day."

The seraphim smiled. "A wise choice."

4. TEN KNIVES

"Ten knives stuck in your back." Savannah stabbed her fingers into Claire's back, causing her to jump a little.

I started paying attention.

"Blood rushing down." She ran her fingers down Claire's back. This time Claire shuddered. Savannah changed her voice to a raspy whisper. "Snakes slithering up. Snakes slithering down. Mice peeping up. Mice peeping down." She carved s-shapes and pinched up and down Claire's back.

It got quiet and heavy in the old jail.

"Spiders crawling up. Spiders crawling down."

I could hear everyone breathing.

"Tight squeeze." She pinched Claire's shoulder. "Cool Breeze." She blew at the back of Claire's neck. "Now, you got the chills."

She pronounced *chills* with the thicker Texan accent as *cheels*. It gave the odd ritual an old-timey sound. We all shivered.

"Ooooo do me," I said to my boyfriend Austin.

"With pleasure." He winked and moved my long hair off my back and I gathered it to one side. He nibbled my exposed neck and gave me goose-pimples before he even started the chant. Austin. I couldn't believe I was dating a guy named *Austin*, ridiculously Texan, and I loved it.

With exception to the rain, things were going better than expected. I'd been planning this for years. When I first laid eyes on the 1908 jail house, I fell in love. It looked like a cowboy castle made of yellow and red brick. I could still hear the aged tour director teaching me the proper description: Norman Castellated architecture. It rose four stories with the top floor resembling a cupola or small penthouse and at some angles it looked like a giant wedding cake.

Small unexplainable incidents had happened through the years I'd volunteered as a docent and gave the tours: cell doors clanged on their own, muted conversations floated from empty cells, gunshots rang at odd times, and smells of baking bread and rosewater perfume wafted through the first floor.

Most of the weirdness could be dismissed as matrixing, but not all. I knew there was something special about the old jail. This being Halloween, I hoped we'd experience something that we'd remember all our lives.

It was only supposed to be the four of us, but Claire's best *cheer* friend, as if you could have a best friend who was a cheerleader, had heard her talking to Harley about it and invited herself, and her boyfriend, Devon. Even though Claire was a cheerleader too, she was different and I couldn't understand how she could be friends with Savannah, but then Claire couldn't understand how I could be friends with all the drama geeks. Still, we were true best friends ever since I'd moved to Texas eight years ago, and she'd never made me feel like an outsider.

"Do you really think it's haunted?" Savannah asked when she arrived.

"Yes, I do, that's why I planned this."

Savanna looked around. "You know, in all the years I've lived here, I've never been to the jail. And I grew up here."

Why did that not surprise me, I thought, but didn't say. I gave a polite nod and looked at Claire who raised her eyebrows. I pasted on a smile and continued with my plan.

"Okay, so no cell phones. I'm going to…"

"What?" Savannah interrupted.

"I'm going to put them all in a drawer. I think it will make the experience creepier. Nothing but flashlights."

"But, what if we see something? We could text you real quick and you could come running," Claire said.

"Hmmm, I hadn't thought of that." I'd wanted it to be really old-fashioned, but she had a point *and* we could take pictures. "Okay, what if NO sound or flash alerts, no surfing or music and only texting to let each other know if you see something?"

"Sounds good." They all agreed. I locked us in and put the keys in my pocket.

We divvied up the three upper levels, skipping the first floor. I was afraid of anyone messing with the collection of antiques, besides Austin kept bugging me about trying out the antique bedroom exhibit.

"Now listen you guys, this is still a museum so, you know, be cool," I said.

"Yes, mother," Devon replied.

"Hey, it's her job, she does work here now," Austin said.

I was proud to have been given the head docent job when Mrs. Acher retired, and Austin sticking up for me made me tingle inside and rethink the eighteen hundred's bedroom exhibit. Doing it for the first time with Austin on Halloween, might be perfect, but I'd think about that later.

I opened the heavy door which led up to the cells. It squeaked like a horror movie sound effect. It was a good way to start. The fellas grabbed the sleeping bags, munchies and beer and followed me up the dirty metal staircase. Cell phone light bounced off the peeling walls, old white paint blistered and shed like a snake shrugging its skin.

"Ack, what was that." Savannah jumped and did a little jig. "I'm not kidding guys, I felt something brush against my leg." All lights converged on the step and wall surrounding her feet.

"I don't see anything," Harley said.

"It was probably some of the wall flaking off, right Molly?" Claire turned her phone light toward me.

"Well maybe. Or maybe, it was a ghost dog, or cat. They would have buried their animals in the courtyard," I replied.

"Oooo, scary, ghost dog," Devon said.

"Um, did you ever read Cujo?" I knew he hadn't read anything outside our English assignments. If he'd even read those.

"Who-jo?" was his brilliant comeback.

"Never mind." We approached the first landing. "But you do know, the sheriff's family used to live here and they might have had a dog or cat. I wonder if animals were allowed inside. I could research that."

"Sure, why not," said Austin. "Seems like everyone back then had house pets, not to mention livestock."

"Not too different from now," Claire added.

I hadn't thought of it that way. That's why Claire and I were best friends. She might be a cheerleader, but she was smarter than all of them put together and had a unique perspective. She thought cheering was just like my acting, only she always played the same character, and the football fans were her audience. Plus, she loved the uniform.

"Well, this is your stop." I pointed my light at Claire and Harley.

Harley looked around. "Well, uh, hey, how about a tour?"

"Not scared are ya?" Savannah teased.

"No," he said, but I detected a little fear under his casual tone. "Like Savannah, I've never been here is all."

"No, a tour's a great idea. Okay, right this way." We walked down a small dark corridor to another set of steps. Our bustling noise sounded like gnawing rats. I showed them into the first room of cells. Devon had to duck not to hit his head.

The rooms had curved ceilings with no sharp corners which gave them an oppressive, underground grotto feel. We sidled through the narrow passage between wall and cells trying not to brush against the corroded bars or the peeling walls.

Savannah and Claire hung back while the guys and I took turns shutting ourselves inside the cells and pretending to eat at the metal table. Austin, Harley and Devon even lay down on the rusted metal bunks, a little too gross even for me. I was glad Austin had short cropped hair, a better chance the rust flakes wouldn't cling and find their way to me.

On our way to the next level I turned my flashlight towards the long wall and dark rectangular shaft. "See that?" I asked.

"Ooo yeah, cool," Devon said, "what is it?"

"It's the dumbwaiter. They used to bring the prisoner's food up here from the downstairs kitchen. Imagine living with, and having to cook for, the criminals and murderers."

"And didn't you tell me three criminals escaped through it in 1958?" Austin asked. I nodded, impressed that he'd remembered.

"Cool, do you think I could fit in it?" Devon walked toward

the crevice.

"No, dumb ass, you're too big," Harley said. Devon was a big guy, fullback for the varsity football team. Even if he could fit, I doubt it could hold his weight.

"Plus, it's rusted solid," Austin answered.

"Damn, that would have been wicked."

We climbed and toured, finally stepping into Solitary Confinement, which was how we all ended up on the top floor playing Ten Knives.

Ten knives stuck in your back
Blood rushing down
Snakes slithering up
Snakes slithering down
Mice peeping up
Mice peeping down
Spiders crawling up
Spiders crawling down
Tight squeeze
Cool breeze
Now you got the chills

We each took turns playing the game, even our guys shivered. When I came to the end of the chant and blew on Austin's neck, a loud crash made us jump.

"What the hell was that?" Savannah asked.

"It sounded like one of the windows," Austin said.

"Oh shit, oh shit," I said. Not on *my* watch, but as the head docent they'd all be *my* watches now.

Austin gave me a pat on the back. "Let's go see." He offered his hand and pulled me up.

"No way, I'm not leaving my spot." Savannah huddled with Claire and squeezed her tight. The rest of us were already on our feet making our way toward the sound of the crash.

"Is it my imagination or did it suddenly get colder in here?" Claire rubbed her arms.

"Nope, not your imagination," Austin said from the other side of the room. "Look at this."

The top half of the double sash window had fallen down and a cool, wet breeze blew through. All three guys took turns trying to close it, but it was stuck open. I was just relieved it wasn't broken, and the little rain that came in couldn't hurt the cement walls and floors, and the bars couldn't get any rustier.

"Okay, enough games, let's get to our levels and do some ghost hunting," I said.

Claire tried to extricate herself from Savannah. "Don't leave me Claire."

"Come on Savannah, you've got Devon, you'll be fine," Claire said.

"No. No. No. I've changed my mind. I don't want to stay. It's too creepy, too cold and," she flicked paint off the rusted bars, "too dirty. I'm sure the rust particles are not good for my lungs. Come on Dev, we're leaving. Molly, let us out." She began shoving her snacks in her bag.

"Well, okay." I wasn't going to talk her into staying. I hadn't wanted her here anyway. Devon rolled up their bags clutching them with one arm, the other arm around Savannah.

"Sorry guys," he said to Austin and Harley. They gave him a nod.

"I thought this would be fun," Savannah continued, "but it's just gross. I don't know what you like about this place Molly. It's a dump. Plus, I didn't think we'd actually be trying to raise any spirits. That just goes against God, you know."

"But you're the one who suggested the Ten Knives game," I said.

"I did not. Claire did."

There was no arguing with her. I rolled my eyes and started down the stairs. This was not going how I wanted, but maybe it would, once she was gone.

"What was that?" Savannah said in a shrill voice.

"I didn't hear anything," Harley said.

"It sounds like water bugs crawling around. I bet this place is infested." Savannah leaned closer to Harley. If he wasn't holding the sleeping bags she might have jumped in his arms.

"You mean cockroaches? We just had the museum sprayed."

"I know what I heard. It sounded like water bugs."

Even after all these years, it was weird but charming, to hear Texans call cockroaches, *water bugs*, maybe it was too un-refined to think anyone who lived in a proper house would have *cockroaches*. In all my volunteering I'd rarely seen a *water bug*, but maybe with the rain? I thought I heard something, too.

"Okay, shhhhh, let me listen."

We froze for a minute on the stairs. A faint sound like dry leaves blowing on pavement pulled our attention. We turned our lights to the floor. Nothing.

The walls. Nothing.

The ceiling. Nothing.

We continued to hear rustling. I inched down the stairs towards the loudest sound. The scritchy-scratch grew loudest at the dumbwaiter and I turned my dim flashlight toward it.

I let out a stifled yelp and dropped my light. It clanked on the metal stairs as Austin raced to my side. "What is it, babe?" he said in hushed tones.

"Um, it's, um, um." I needed to get a grip. It was no big deal. It was only that there were so many of them. "Um, slowly turn your light toward the dumbwaiter, but put it on the lowest setting, you don't want to disturb them."

"Holy shit," he whispered.

"What's going on down there?" Claire and Harley edged down the stairs and squeezed in tight behind us.

"What the hell?" Harley said.

"We're never going to get Savannah past them," I whispered. "I'm not afraid, but there are so many."

"What's going on down there?" Savannah asked in a squeaky little girl voice. I almost felt sorry for her, almost.

"Look it's um, it's um a nest of…" I began.

Austin clamped his hand over my mouth. "She'll freak," he whispered in my ear.

"What do you suggest?" I hissed back.

"Let's play a game," Austin said. "Um, it's called... *Leading the Blind*. The girls have to close their eyes and trust their boyfriends to lead them."

Quicker on the uptake than me, Claire jumped in, "I love that game, we used to play it at Sunday School. Remember Savannah." I looked at her; she shrugged and gestured to play along.

"No, I don't remember," Savannah answered.

"Sure, come on, one last fun game. It's Halloween and all," Claire said.

"Yeah, come on Savannah." Everyone jumped in, cajoling her to play.

"Okay. Okay. I'll play."

We lined up at the edge of the rail, pressing our bodies into the cool metal bar, the scritchy-scratch rustling louder.

"Keep your flashlights on the ground so we don't trip," I said in a fake cheerful voice.

Austin and I were almost to the next stairwell when a beam of light hit the nest and all hell broke loose. Savannah cheated and flashed her phone light, on the brightest setting, at the dumbwaiter. Then let out a blood curdling scream.

The spiders erupted and began crawling over the walls and floor, pouring out of the dark crevice. We all ran like hell.

Above the sound of a million scurrying legs, the crunch of

exoskeletons snapped in our ears as we slipped and scrambled on spider guts. The horde jumped and flung themselves at us as we ran. We worked as a team, swatting them away and knocking them off the person in front of us.

Somehow Savannah managed to get by us all without pushing anyone down. By the time we reached the first floor I was damp with sweat and my heart was racing, but I was laughing. We were all perfectly fine.

"Are you laughing at me?" Savannah said.

"No, I'm laughing at us, being afraid of a few spiders."

"There was more than a few and they were huge," Devon said.

"Well, this is Texas. Nobody got bit did they?" I asked.

"Just let us out." Savannah stomped her foot.

I reached in my pocket and they weren't there. I checked my other pocket. "Austin, did I give you my keys?"

"That's not funny, Molly, I want to go," Savannah said crossing her arms and pouting.

"I'm not being funny. They must have fallen out of my pocket in our mad dash to freedom," I said and laughed again.

"It's not funny." She looked near tears.

I rolled my eyes and turned on my heels, retracing my steps, scanning the floor for keys. Austin followed, followed by Claire, Harley and Devon.

"Devon, don't leave me here all alone."

"Well, the sooner we find the keys, the sooner we can go.

More eyes looking is better. Come help."

"No, I'm not going. I'm staying right here, by this door. Please don't leave me."

Devon sighed and resigned. "Whatever you say, babe." He circled his finger in *she's crazy* gesture and pointed back toward Savannah, then headed her way.

The door creaked again when I opened it and this time I shivered. We crept up the steps and shifted our lights across the stairs, walls, and ceiling. My heart beat faster with each step toward the nest. We made the landing where they'd poured out and flashed our lights. I thought I caught movement in the dumbwaiter, but nothing. We continued up to Solitary, thinking maybe I'd dropped the keys there.

That's when we heard it: two long, low screeches. At first I thought it was an owl outside the open window; then, I recognized the pitch of Savannah's whine.

"Should we go see?" I asked.

"She's got Devon with her." Austin shrugged.

"Something just doesn't feel right," Claire said.

"You don't think…" I said.

"The spiders?" we said and headed for the stairs. This time I wasn't laughing. When we reached the ground floor there was no sound. I was the first one to round the corner.

"Oh my god." I stopped. Austin, Claire, and Harley filed in around me.

"We have to call the police." Claire turned off her phone's

flashlight and began dialing 911.

"Are they still breathing?" Austin asked.

I didn't want to touch them. They were covered in pimpled red welts, with pus oozing out the middle. Savannah's arms and feet were covered in sores, and I could see dark splotches on her jeans where they must have bitten through the fabric. The worst were their faces. Devon's had swelled to almost twice its size, and Savannah's looked like a pink tomato, their expressions frozen in terror.

"I don't have any cell phone service," Claire held up her phone, angling it toward the window.

"What?" I asked.

"My cell phone. I don't have any service."

Austin and Harley looked at their phones.

"Shit, mine's dead, too." Harley frowned.

"Mine, too." Austin popped his battery out and put it back in. "Nothing."

"Well, you were using the flashlights a lot, they do drain the battery," I said and edged around the bodies to the desk.

A hairy spider crawled out of Savannah's mouth. I tasted bile at the back of my throat and forgot for a second what I was doing.

"We can uh, use the old-fashioned land-line." I picked up the receiver. "Um, it's dead, too."

Just then the thunder cracked and the museum was plunged into darkness. I shook my flashlight and re-activated its battery. It wasn't as bright as a regular flashlight, but it was a light in the dark. I grabbed the other flashlights from the drawer and handed them out.

"Look, this is no game. We need to get out of here," Harley said.

"And how do you propose we do that? The door is locked with a deadbolt that only a key will open and all the windows have bars." I rubbed my temples in frustration. "Look, I'm sorry to be snappy. This is wrong, all wrong. I just wanted to have a little ghost adventure for Halloween is all, maybe make contact."

"Well, you can't choose your ghosts." Claire shook her flashlight; it emitted a dim light.

"You think this was ghosts?" I pointed at Devon and Savannah.

"Yeah, what do you think it was?" Claire said.

"Spiders? We all saw the spiders." I looked around.

"When have you ever seen spiders like that, and attacking like a swarm?" Harley asked.

"I don't know. This is Texas." My head was spinning.

"Okay, let's retrace your steps; we have to find the keys," Austin said.

"Maybe they got rolled up in their sleeping bags?"

"Good idea Claire. I'll check 'em." Austin unrolled each bag and shook it, but no keys dropped out. "Did you set them down, go to the bathroom?" he asked.

"Let's just go upstairs and look again," Harley said.

"Hey, the window, it's open and there are no bars on the

windows in Solitary." Claire shook her flashlight harder. The beam brightened.

"Oh, yes, you're brilliant Claire, let's go." I gave her a hug.

We trudged our way up the stairs and back to Solitary. It had gotten colder and smelled strongly of rotting apples. I was accustomed to the musty smells of the place, but this was strange. I thought maybe it was coming from the jail's next door neighbor, Livengood Feeds, but that didn't make any sense either.

Harley boosted Claire up to the window opening. She wedged her head out the window but had no way to maneuver her legs to land. We pulled her back through. She came up with a plan, a reverse cheer-stunt. By putting her hands on Harley's shoulders, Austin and I were able to guide her legs feet-first through the window. She landed effortlessly with a soft bounce and disappeared around the corner. Austin and Devon did the same maneuver with me, only I was less coordinated than Claire. My feet slid ungracefully on the wet roof like a giraffe on ice.

I edged my way around to the protected side and found Claire peering over the edge. I could tell by her look of concentration she was trying to work out a way down.

"Hey, help me out over here. I'm out, but Harley's stuck," Austin yelled.

The rain grew angrier with pelting, stinging drops. I wiped clinging hair out of my eyes as Claire and I went back to the window. We found Harley doing a handstand with the bottom of his legs poking out the window.

"Help me hold his legs." Austin grabbed one, Claire and I the other. "Pull."

I thought we were going to break his back, but we got him through and all shuffled back to the sheltered side of Solitary.

Austin had the brilliant idea of scrambling down the brick face. He'd done a lot of spelunking and thought he could manage the climb, but as he lay on his stomach with his feet hung over the edge, the rain made it too slippery for any kind of foothold. He even took off his shoes and though he had a little more control, he couldn't get enough purchase in the brick façade to climb down.

We rested and regrouped, our backs against the damp outside wall of Solitary. I felt Claire shaking beside me and realized she was crying, too. Our tears mixed with the biting rain, we reached out and clasped hands. Our boyfriends pulled us closer to them and tried to comfort us. I rested my head on Austin's shoulder and wept, cuddling next to his warm body until my tears were done.

A bright light flashed almost simultaneously as the thunder cracked. We instinctively reached to cover our ears and closed our eyes. When I reopened them, the fireworks from the blown transformer were sparking out. The entire town, as far as we could see, was plummeted into darkness.

My hope of trying to flag a late-night driver was dashed. It was a longshot that anyone would look up, but now it was too dark to see us if they did.

Through the rain I smelled the rotten apple scent again, and saw a dark mass undulating toward us. I jumped to my feet as the pack of mice and rats began to crawl up my shoe. I shook off the first, jumping and slipping on the oily roof. Claire and Harley were closest to the roiling pack and the first to be attacked. Harley jumped in front of Claire helping her bat them down. Tiny teeth pinched through my shoes and jeans. My hands throbbed with open wounds.

The vermin made their way up Harley's body. He became a gray mass of wriggling wet fur, only his head and hands visible. Somehow he continued to beat them off Claire, but he had backed too close to the edge. Claire tried to reach out and grab him, but the rats piled atop his body tipping him over the edge.

"I love you Claire," he cried as his arms flapped in mid-air for a second before gravity pulled him downward. She started to go after him but slipped, and I grabbed her before she could follow him over. We barely heard the thud as Harley hit the ground. In unison, the rats and mice scrabbled over the edge and down the wall. I had no stomach to watch what happened next.

Claire and I clung to each other shaking. "I want to go home. I want to go home." She repeated over and over. "I want to go home."

Somehow Austin got us back through the window. We stripped off our wet pants and shirts, and huddled in our sleeping bags. We tried to get Claire to drink some beer to warm her up faster, but she refused and continued to wobble, reciting her chorus of *I want to go home.*

At some point I must have fallen asleep and awoke with a jolt. Austin slept next to me, but when I looked at Claire's sleeping bag, it was empty. I shook Austin awake. The funk of stale beer clung to his skin, and a can rattled as he stood up. He must have continued drinking after we'd fallen asleep. He was groggy and disoriented, but still so very handsome.

I couldn't help notice how good he looked in his underwear. I knew lust and love were different, and recognized what I felt as lust, but underneath it, I also realized I loved this man. If I wasn't so worried about Claire I would have asked him to make love to me right there, instead I said, "Claire's missing."

He ran his fingers over his cropped hair and reached for his jeans, but decided they were too wet to get on. I couldn't help notice he glanced at me from head to toe. It had been the right choice to wear my prettiest bra and panty set. I blushed a little under his gaze and felt my body warm.

He adjusted his underwear and mumbled something I couldn't hear.

"Claire! Claire!" We both shouted as we worked our way down the levels, checking every room. I wanted to find Claire, but I was acutely aware of Austin's bare body next to mine. Why it was different than being in a swimming pool I didn't know, but I wanted to put my hands on his skin, maybe re-assure myself he was real and we were alive.

Electricity crackled between us. Before we hit the second floor I leaned into him and kissed him hard. He kissed me back and gathered me in his arms, rubbing down my back, pulling my hips toward him. "I'd love to continue this, but should we look for Claire or not?" he asked in a thick voice.

"Yes," I whispered as I tore myself away from him. "Claire!" I yelled.

"I gotta use the john," he said as we hit the first floor. I walked with him to the bathroom and just as Austin reached for the knob the door opened.

"Claire. I've never been so happy to see you." I gave her a hug. "Feeling okay?"

Austin slipped into the bathroom while I questioned Claire.

"As okay as I can feel. I think we're going to make it. Everything will be okay in the morning," she answered.

I didn't want to say it wouldn't be okay, it would never be okay, but she wasn't acting crazy, so I'd take it.

"Do you smell that?" Claire asked.

"The funny, musky, metallic smell?"

"It smells a little bit like when the pilot light goes out."

"What's taking Austin so long in the..."

"What the..." Austin said from behind the closed door. Then something that sounded like silk fabric being rubbed together overtook every other noise in the jail. I pounded on the door. "Austin! Open up! Open up!"

I ran to the glass case with the display of skeleton keys and grabbed them all. I shoved each one into the old keyhole of the bathroom door until I found the one that fit. The door swung open.

The rotting putrid stench almost knocked me down and made me vomit. Wriggling snakes wrapped his body like a mummy. Blood seeped between slithering coils, bitten flesh flashed and gaped, pink and slimy. I didn't know anything about snakes or if these were poisonous, but they wrapped around his neck and over his mouth like a gag. His eyes and crop spike of hair were still visible and his eyes were pleading.

Claire grabbed the fire extinguisher and started blasting the snakes with it, trying to avoid Austin's face. Austin saw it coming and closed his eyes. I wasn't sure he could breathe but he got what we were doing and managed to turn his back to us. Claire continued to blast the CO as Austin slowly collapsed. We had to get him out of there. Ice crystals formed on the snakes and they began retreating, crawling into the toilet and down the drain, liquid silver running backwards.

As soon as most were dead or disappearing, Claire and I rushed in and each grabbed an arm, sliding Austin across the dying snakes and foam. His body was riddled with scores of punctures, each one oozing bright red blood. He remained unconscious. I said a quick prayer, hoping they had not been venomous.

I shut the door, locked it, retrieved Savannah's sleeping bag, and shoved it under the door making sure to fill the space.

"Good idea," Claire said.

"You had the great idea to use the fire extinguisher. Way to think fast."

"Well, we'd just used them to make dry ice in Ms. Thurhill's chem class."

"Class. School. Seems like another world. Some parallel universe we used to exist in."

"Yeah, I don't know if I can go back to school." Claire shook her head.

"I can't think about any of that right now. I'm going to…."

"Ow," Claire cried out and jerked her body forward. A large dark stain spread across the back yoke of her shirt.

"Oh Claire, you must've cut yourself."

Silent tears ran down her cheeks. I gave her a quick hug and said, "I'm going to go to the kitchen to get some rags and paper towels, and the first aid kit. Are you okay if I leave you?"

"I don't know." She pulled her knees to her body and started rocking back and forth. She whispered something, but I couldn't hear what she said. I didn't want to leave her, but had to get something to stanch the cut.

I was only gone five minutes, but when I returned she was on her side in a fetal position. More red blotches marked her back; blood pooled on the floor next to her. It was too much blood. I didn't remember her getting bit by any of the snakes, but the assault had happened so fast, it was possible.

I got Devon's sleeping bag and spread it next to her. "Claire, I'm going to roll you to your stomach." I straightened her legs and eased her over, my hands slipped and smeared the globs of blood.

I tried to mop her back with the kitchen rags, but the gashes were too numerous and the blood kept coming.

Then I had an idea. I laid several layers of blood soaked rags on her back and grabbed the fire-extinguisher hoping there was enough CO left. Claire moaned when I pulled the trigger but didn't move. It looked like I had successfully frozen her back and the bleeding had stopped. How long that would last I didn't know.

"Claire. Claire. Can you hear me?" I brushed her hair off her face. She moaned and mouthed words. "What? I'm sorry, I can't hear you."

"Ten. Knives," she whispered.

Oh my god, ten knives. And that's when I felt the first stab in my back.

Tam Francis

5. CLOUDS AND RAIN

Blood dripped from the mattress like syrup. It wasn't supposed to be like this. His work shirt clung to his body and sweat trickled down his pale brow. His bare arms and hands were stained with her blood, oil and excrement. He sat motionless, not sure what to do next.

It wasn't supposed to be like this. He'd gone to the library and read the medical books. He'd researched for months and learned how to do it. He was sure he could. Ester had trusted him, had faith in him. No hospital would take her. No doctor would come. She was a woman of color, descended from slaves, he, Fergus, was a pale Irish immigrant. He boiled the water from the well, sharpened his best fillet knife and bought a block of ice.

They'd both scrubbed the grubby shack from floor to ceiling.

He never thought they'd end up in a shack, but she had stuck with him when the market crashed and the depression deepened. He'd lost everything but her. If only he'd had more money. But no one would take the risk, not in the Deep South, and not without a lot of cash.

It wasn't supposed to be like this.

His wife lay dying. She had stopped fighting. She had stopped pushing. Her eyes had rolled back into her head and were still. Her bloody, sweat-soaked body laid inert, save for the rhythmic contractions, a wave of flesh rippling across her bulbous belly and a slow, shallow breath. He did not know how much time they had. If the books were to be believed, minutes. Only minutes.

Her hips were too slim. He'd tried everything he'd learned in the medical books, but he wasn't a doctor. He massaged her with oil and fed her ice chips to keep away dehydration and vomiting. They had tried every position: standing, squatting, prone. A steady stream of blood poured out of her, and her body refused to open, until she was shattered and could take no more.

The heat and darkness of the shack pressed in on him like a coffin.

It wasn't supposed to be like this.

Suddenly, he noticed the shadows shift and change. His wife's brown skin glowed with reflected light. He turned to his left and saw her standing there, but not there. He recognized her caramel skin and beautiful body. Her black ringlets hung loose and free, how he imagined she'd looked as a girl, instead of the tight fingerwaves that usually framed her lovely face. But he could also see the back of the shack, the small window opened to the dark night. He reached out and put his hand right through her middle.

"Cut me," she said. As her lips moved, her voice resonated in his head rather than his ears.

He looked from the body of his wife to the figure at his side. He was sure he'd gone insane. He'd read about that too, but he knew in his soul this was no hallucination. The spirit of his wife looked at him and herself. But she wasn't dead. She wasn't dead. She wasn't dead. He could still see the slight rise and fall of her chest and the contractions roll across her body.

"It isn't supposed to be like this," he said aloud.

"It is, it was, it will be," she replied.

And then he remembered. A year ago, before he'd lost everything, he'd bolted awake from sleep. His heart hurtling in his chest, a pain ached in his center, his skin crawled with fear. He gazed at his wife, her body curled next to his, her silky rayon gown draped like mist over her brown body. He ran his hand over her thin arm and laid his head on her hip, trying to get the nightmare out of his head. He let his head rise and fall with her even breathing. The dream faded and he went back to sleep, never to think of it until now.

In his dream, Ester had stood before him, her hair in wild curls. A knife in each hand, the blades glistened and dripped dark blood, pooling around her feet. She had spoken those words. "It is, it was, it will be."

※ ※ ※

"Cut me," Ester's apparition said again at his side.

"I can't. I can't. I love you. You are my life."

"I am no longer life, but take the life we made. Take it, before it is too late."

He stared at her. All of his love for her swirled inside him. He was full, yet empty. Tears ran down his cheeks. He thought of the first time he'd seen her.

※ ※ ※

She stood behind the microphone, her lilac dress wrapped around her hips and breasts, just tight enough that it tugged the fabric. He pictured his big freckled hands gathering the fabric in his fists and pulling it over her head.

When he finally did, he was surprised to see the white blotches across her belly and thighs, like spilled bleach where no pigment colored her dark skin. Her hands were afflicted too, and he understood why she'd always worn gloves. In their passionate frenzy she'd forgotten her shame, then remembered it, and tried to hide herself, turning her back to him, and tucking her hands under the pillow.

"You're beautiful," he said and turned her around, pulling her hands from under the pillow, holding them with his. "My gal has clouds across her body. The heavens have come out of the sky and touched her."

She smiled and let him run his hand across her clouds.

"And my fella has been touched by the heavens as well. Dark raindrops have decorated your skin with stars."

She ran her hands over his freckled face, touching one of the millions of dots that he always thought looked like splattered mud. He'd hated them, but seen through her eyes, he was breathtaking. She ran her hand from his face to his arm, tracing the line of brown spots down one arm and up the other. Then across his chest, stomach and thighs. No skin on his body was unspeckled. She touched them all, and then proceeded to kiss them each.

※ ※ ※

"It isn't supposed to be like this," he said aloud, again.

"We are losing time. Cut me," she begged.

"I can't."

At once the room became dim, almost black by contrast. His warm body felt like it was on fire—heat so hot it felt like ice. He had no control of his limbs and his vision grew filmy. He watched as his hands reached out and grabbed the knife from the table. His white skin looked like moonlight and emanated a soft glow.

The sharp blade made a sucking, sickening sound like gutting fish, as it cut into her belly. The flesh fell open in spongy layers. She in command of his being, sliced through the embryonic sac and set the knife on the table next to the block of ice. It smeared in the pool of overflowing melt.

With his hands she groped for the tiny bloody body inside of her. One hand cupped around the baby's head, the other around its bottom, and yanked it free. She set the bloody bundle on his lap, grabbed the knife, and cut the cord. She cleared the mouth and nose, cleaning the babe and swaddling it, setting the baby boy in the basket. He cried loud and strong, filling the hut with a hurricane of sound.

Fergus thought she would leave him then, leave him for good, but he watched again as his puppeted arms yanked another babe from the bloody slit and repeated the procedure. The baby girl howled louder than her brother.

His body convulsed as Ester expelled herself from him. This time he did feel like ice, the deepest, coldest ice of a sunless universe, the coldness of eternity, of time and space. And then it was gone. She was gone from him. He wept with all the love he had, all the love he'd lost and all the love never to be.

The room glowed bright again. Her dead body wore her spectral one like a shroud and her ghost figure floated a whisper above its corporeal counterpart. Fergus reached out to touch her cold hand and found it warm. More than warm. Hot. The heat continued to rise until he could no longer bear to hold it. Her brightness grew so dazzling he had to turn his eyes away. Flames began to dance on her skin.

He scrambled back, picked up the basket with the babes

and walked toward the door. The fire consumed her body, the bed and licked up the walls. He stopped in the firelight for a second to inspect the newborns.

A perfectly acceptable color, with a shock of red hair. Not as pale as he, and not as dark as her. He could raise them anywhere. They could go anywhere. Sit anywhere. Be anyone they wanted to be. Grow up outside the walls of prejudice. No one would know their mother had been Negro. But he would tell the twins. And they would know of their mother, the woman who danced with the clouds, the rain, and the stars.

Tam Francis

6. DRESSING THE PART

Lizzy closed her eyes and tried to find her partner's rhythm; it often helped when dancing with a stranger. She didn't know what possessed her to sign up for the Jack and Jill contest. She hadn't been dancing very long and Jack and Jill contests could be particularly difficult. Paired with a random partner and rotated every ninety seconds, she'd be judged on how well she followed and how much individual style she could add to the dance. Still in the first round, she couldn't feel his lead, so she closed her eyes.

She shifted into the past, like a memory she'd never had, and found herself jitterbugging with a leggy sailor at a USO dance. His rough hands chafed hers, but she liked his enthusiasm and joy of dance. She smiled and followed his lead—his rhythm solid and easy. When Lizzy opened her eyes, she found herself back in present time, her lanky partner smiling at her. She'd found his rhythm. When he spun her out of the Shadow Charleston, it felt good. If the judges were paying attention they would've noticed she hadn't missed a step.

She guessed it was her new vintage dress. The 1940's era, poufy sleeve, A-line skirt in pink umbrellas, and black trim made her feel more graceful. She'd finally found the courage to dress the part. Not all the swing dancers did, but she admired the winners of the national contest, and they'd worn vintage clothing. It made the Lindy Hop seem that much more authentic. She didn't know how to do her hair or make-up yet, but when she'd stopped by an estate sale in her neighborhood, the dresses called to her. She was thrilled to find they were her size. Even more astonishing, a pair of wedgie shoes that matched all three dresses, fit perfectly as well.

She'd had the dresses dry-cleaned and she'd worn one for the first time tonight. It boosted her confidence enough to sign up for the contest.

A thin sheath of perspiration covered her body. The dress clung to her like a second skin, and she felt strangely invincible. She made it through to the next level. All the leads in the final round were good and solid but led complicated moves she didn't know. She followed the flow of the dress, the skirt wrapped around her thighs like a Morning Glory. The poufy sleeve kept her from raising her arm too high, which would have resulted in elbowing her fourth partner in the face.

They announced Lizzy as the winning Jill, surprising her, but another part of her was smug with the win. Emboldened from her success she found herself asking all the hotshot dancers to dance. Once or twice, naughty thoughts about the guy at the end of her arm entered her mind. She'd never thought that way about a stranger before. Visceral flashes of flesh popped before her eyes. It was as if she was of two minds. She danced every song until the lights went up and the organizers ushered everyone out.

She hadn't felt the blisters from the new old shoes until she got home and peeled off her socks. The cotton stuck to the raw circles of rubbed flesh. Luckily there was no blood.

He dipped her and pressed his leg between hers, closer than most leads would. She didn't mind, liking the way her dress slid across her hips and trailed to the floor. His breath ghosted across her neck. She wanted him. And when he pulled her up from the dip, she shifted her weight and leaned into his taut body, aware of the thin rayon fabric between them. She'd seen him before and thought he was cute, but had never danced with him before tonight.

His jet-black hair was slicked into a 1930's gangster coif, a few strands had fallen over his dark eyes. High Korean cheekbones hid a shadow of acne scars, and only a few inches taller than she, his athletic body fit hers like a mirror image. He smiled.

"I thought you were a beginner dancer. That was a kick ass

dance. You dance like you've been dancing for years," he said, low in her ear, not releasing her from their close position. "Thanks for my best dance of the night."

Other partners were breaking apart, grabbing their coats and bags, he and Lizzy held fast to each other.

"You're welcome," she answered, stressing the word *welcome*. Lizzy didn't feel like herself exactly, but she liked the way she felt. Bold.

"So, are you hungry?" he asked.

"Hmmm, very."

"Well, would you like to go grab something to eat? I think a bunch of the other dancers are heading to the diner." She shrugged, looked him up and down, then raised her brows.

"Or, I could fix something for us at my place? We Asians are good cooks, you know." He winked.

"That sounds swell. I love Chop Suey." She wondered why she said that, she'd never had Chop Suey, and she'd never used the world *swell* before, though it reminded her of an old movie. "I'll follow you in my car," she added.

❀ ❀ ❀

The dim hallway light cast a warm glow across their bodies as they scrambled through the doorway. He pulled the keys from the lock and shut the door with a swift kick. Lizzy grabbed his face and pulled it to hers, smashing her mouth into his. He tossed his keys on the chair and returned her kiss, pulling her tight. She backed him against the wall, knocking a lamp to the floor on her way. She tugged at his shirt, pulling it over his head between kisses, and ran her hands down his smooth creamy chest.

"I don't even know your name," he said between kisses.

"Betty," Lizzy said. Though her name was Elizabeth, she'd always been Lizzy. She was distracted by the vibrations zooming through her body. His body was young and firm and she wanted all of it.

"I'm Wayne. How do you get this damn thing off?" he said as he groped the back of her dress for a zipper.

"Oh, it's vintage, the zipper's on the side." He slid the fastener down and pulled the dress over her head.

As soon as her dress was off, he turned her against the wall and pressed his body into hers, running his hands over her breasts, waist, and hips. Instead of wanting more, her body and mind started to cool. He grabbed the edge of her slip and tugged it toward her head.

"Whoa, we're moving a little fast," she said and smoothed down the garment.

He took a step back. "Uh, okay, I was just following your lead."

"Yeah, I know." She kissed him softly, the lust gone, only a low simmer remained. "I just got crazy for a minute, and I don't want to rush things. I really like you, and I really am hungry."

He exhaled with a puff and ran his hands through his hair.

"Well, okay, food it is. How about pancakes?"

"Not very Asian," she smiled, "but it sounds good."

❦ ❦ ❦

She looked at her face in the mirror and finally began to recognize herself. She'd dyed the hair red, cut it shoulder length, and pulled it up into victory rolls. Curls bounced around her neck. Once the brows and eyelashes were touched up she brushed jungle-red lipstick across the lips. The new brassieres really pushed up her boobs and made her waist look even smaller. She wasn't crazy about the tight panties, but she'd get used to them. She was going to live it up, and do everything her heart desired, and that pesky girl was not going to stop her.

When she arrived at the bar, the band had already played halfway into their first set. Her new friends greeted her, and Wayne wasted no time pulling her onto the dance floor.

"I like the new hair. Looks good against your skin."

"It would look even better against yours," she said.

"Hmmm, would it?" He nuzzled her neck and kissed behind her ear, dragging his lips across her earlobe before he sent her out into a spin. She tingled from ear to toes and back again.

Her vintage dress, the third in her collection, clung to her body and rushed around her legs like river water, the blue gabardine fabric accented the thumping bass. Wayne slid his hand from her back to her hip, pressing into her firm curve. Not a jitterbug move, but she liked it. She smiled and caught his eye when she came around from a shoulder-twist turn, spinning a full three-hundred-and-sixty degrees. She hadn't felt so alive in years.

When the dance was over she was ready to go home with

him and pick up where they'd left off, but the night was young, and anticipation made the game that much more fun. She wouldn't make the same mistake as last time and let him take the dress off. She thought she could be very creative with her favorite 40s dress. Before he could walk her off the floor, a nerdy guy with pleated pants and a button-down, short sleeve shirt, came running up to them.

"Hi Lizzy," the nerdy guy said in a wispy high-pitched voice.

"Lizzy? I thought it was..." Wayne said.

"Betty. I go by Betty now, Garth."

"Oh, that's odd." Garth cocked his head like a parrot, contemplated this information and continued with his overzealous address. "Well, I'm back from my vacation. It's great to see you out. Glad to see you stuck with the jitterbug. It was sure great meeting you in that Lindy Hop class. Would you like to dance?"

She wanted to say no. She wanted to stay with Wayne and join her new group of cool jitterbug friends. She wanted to tell him to scram, but something inside her made her smile and answer, "Sure Garth, I'd love to dance with you."

It was like dancing with a metronome, on the beat, but no zest and on his toes like a prancing pony. She couldn't sink into any of her favorite moves and wondered how she'd befriended him at the dance lesson. He led switches, and she rotated around him like a satellite, her feet playing with the clarinet solo.

"Whoa, that's fancy. When did you learn that? You got good, fast," he said.

"Thank you." She half-smiled, but couldn't wait for the dance to be over.

As she came around for the turn, her zipper placket caught on one of his buttons. There was no way she could hear the seam rip over the sound of the band, but somehow, she did. It sounded like rapid gunfire and as the shots echoed in her ears, she miscalculated a step, twisted her foot, and folded onto the floor.

"Nooooooo," Betty said.

"Oh Lizzy, I mean Betty. Oh, I'm so sorry. Are you okay?"

"Yes. No. Yes. Lizzy. Yes. Call me, Lizzy." Tears streamed down her face.

"Oh, no. Don't cry. Let's get you some ice."

"No, really. I'm okay," she said, unbuckling her vintage wedgie shoes. The fresh blister stuck to the old leather and pulled away. Blood trickled onto the parquet floor.

"Chhhh, fff, bllrrr," Betty couldn't form words in Lizzy's mouth.

"Your dress. I'm sorry. I'll pay for it," Garth said. "You just take it to a tailor and..."

"Shhhh. It's okay. I'm grateful." It was like speaking from the bottom of a well, but Lizzy could speak again. She looked down at the ripped seam. It ran almost to the hem of the dress. "Garth, can you grab my coat?" She pointed to the chair.

He ran over and retrieved Lizzy's coat. "Can you find

Wayne and tell him about our accident. Tell him I'll call him later?"

She hobbled as fast as she could to the bathroom and slammed the door to the stall, tearing at the beautiful vintage dress. It ripped clear up the side. She slid her arms out and let it drop to the floor. Something inside her tore at the same time. She convulsed and leaned over the toilet and vomited until she was empty.

Her coat was too warm and felt itchy against her skin, but she buttoned it over her slip and picked up the dress. Now that she recognized it, she could feel the energy emanating from the dress like small static shocks, little bits of Betty trying to push back in. The water from the sink tasted like minerals, but was refreshing as she rinsed her mouth and dabbed her neck and temples with the cold water.

It was a strange sight to see herself as a redhead. She liked the hair style though, very 1940's, pulled up in rolls, arched eyebrows and a pretty silk flower at her ear. As much as she hated Betty for taking over her body and trying to bury Lizzy inside, a small part of her would be forever changed. The red would have to go, though.

The darling wedgie shoes had to go, too. She took a knife to them, piercing the leather like an animal. She pulled, and tore, and ravaged the shoes until they were unrecognizable. With the demolition of each vintage items she felt further and further away from Betty and more like Lizzy. She thought about writing it down or telling someone, but no one would believe her. She barely believed it herself. Looking back, Lizzy could see how Betty had slowly poured into her every time she wore one of Betty's dresses. She didn't understand it, but knew somehow Betty's soul was in the clothes.

She cried as she cut the beautiful fabric into tiny pieces. She cried for the loss of the connection to the past. She cried for the loss of Betty's jitterbug knowledge and the hours of practice it would take to be as good as Betty. But mostly, she cried for never ever having felt as confident, beautiful, and wonderful as Betty had made her feel. She cried because she didn't know when she would feel like that again, if ever.

When she was done with the dissection, she took the parts to the fire pit in the apartment commons. The dress pieces fell like flower petals onto the ash pile. She'd bought two things on her way home, one of them lighter fluid, which she squirted onto the heap.

She dropped a lit match; it ignited with a whoosh and in the crackling blaze she was sure she could hear a trumpet, clarinet, and bass beat out a solid rhythm. She cried for the joy of dance, and jitterbugged around the firelight until it smoldered into a million glowing eyes.

Lizzy went inside, read the directions inside the box of hair dye, and smiled.

7. THE TOUR

ow do they live without their bodies?" I asked. It wasn't that I was disturbed by their grotesque gray heads, which looked a cross between ancient Asian warriors and boars heads. It wasn't the way the heads bobbed and hopped independent of arms and legs like Mexican jumping beans. It wasn't their foul smell of newly rotting compost. No, what disturbed me was what they ate and how they defecated. As any other boy of fourteen will tell you (maybe not as intelligently as me), all things scatological are an endless form of fascination and hilarity.

"There are many different types of existence. These I collected from the Far East. They live much like epiphytes or perhaps it is parasites. I often get the two confused," he replied. His dark cape trailed him like a snail. "Although, I doubt it matters, really."

My guide's voice had an echo quality, like it wasn't coming from his mouth, but everywhere, outside and inside my head at the same time.

"What are they? I've never seen anything like them. They're pretty wicked," I said.

"Yes, yes, well, how clever of you, they are indeed the heads of the Wicked Oni. I considered bringing back the bodies as well, but they're too rambunctious and hard to keep fed. The heads though, they're much more easily sated."

"What do they do?"

"Do?" he said with a hint of amusement in his hollow voice, "they do what they all do."

He swept his cloaked arm through the thick dark air. I couldn't wait to see what else was there. So far I'd observed nothing scarier than monsters in video games and movies. I turned my head and rolled my eyes, not impressed. Still, I was hopeful that there would be something I could sink my teeth into, so to speak.

His long gray robes sailed behind him and billowed forward as he walked silently, my footfalls crunching loudly on the rocky path. The hood, which encased his face, was so deep I could see only the palest outline of a skull, a skull I wasn't even sure was human. I wasn't scared though. I, Edward Vilhelm Longgate, (known as Eddy), wasn't scared a nothing...anything.

The closest I came to being scared was running into that

kid Thurston. Not that he was big or scary or he could take me in a fight. No, it was quite the opposite. We called him Turdston. He had a perpetual runny nose and floppy hair that grated on my nerves like an empty stomach. His very existence in the world made me uneasy, uncomfortable. How could anyone be that frail, that pathetic and be *my* age.

He gave me the creeps and once that feeling got going it just kept growing like those multiplying cells in biology. It got bigger and bigger and nothing would make it go away until I sunk my fist into his puny offending body. It wasn't that I wanted him to give me his lunch money or something. I just had to shake the creeps off me and laying him flat made me feel calm and solid.

"And here we have one of my personal favorites," he spoke again, stopping at another murky grotto.

We walked down a bit and I couldn't see anything but dark. The whole place was pitch black. It was disappointing, just like the zoo. The tigers or silver back gorillas, the animals you really wanted to see, were always hiding behind a big tree or fake rock made to look like a termite mound. Nothing to see. I was getting bored. I shrugged my shoulders.

"Ah, you have to be patient. My Antigora shows herself only when she's ready to feed."

"Feed? But not on us?" I asked, alarmed for a millisecond before regaining my cool.

I wasn't a hundred percent, but I was pretty sure, that there was nothing to fear here. I didn't get the creepy feeling, not like when old man Mooney would limp off his porch and totter down his sidewalk to collect his mail. I couldn't stand that old man. My ma told me, (before she left), that he'd been a famous wrestler, one of those guys who wore shiny underpants, broke chairs over heads and pile-drove opponent's skulls into mats like potato mashers.

I couldn't picture it. He was aged and withered. Every time I saw his crooked walk or heard his wheezy laugh, I would wish him dead. I hated looking at him. I would never end up that frail. It would be a kindness if someone smothered his wrinkly old face with a soft downy pillow while he slept. Then I wouldn't have the creepy feeling that made my stomach sour, my heart beat fast and my breath feel thin.

Even though I was out of my element and wasn't sure how I got to this place, or why I was here, nothing I'd seen gave me the feeling old man Mooney or Turdston gave me. Nah, this tour was like a rollercoaster, sitting at the top, just about to drop down the scary slope for the big thrill at the end of the ride.

"Not feed on us, right?" I repeated just to be sure.

"Feed? On us? No. No, not on—*us*," said my guide in reply to the question I wished I could take back. Of course not on us, how could I have said something so dumb.

I leaned into the blackness willing my eyes to see something that might make me feel—anything. I liked roller coasters.

To the right a vague outline of a dark figure curved in the

corner, a hint of light glinted off a shimmering edge. It might have been a trick of my eyes. That's when it attacked from the left. I threw myself backwards. Stumbled across the rough path. Two large fangs poised at my throat. Gigantic prickly legs froze in midair. I quickly counted eight.

I took a deep breath, blinked my eyes and glared into its gaping maw. Silken threads, wispy as whispers, hung about its mouth. It struck. I waited for the pain, not afraid. Pain was nothing to me, but none came. It struck again and again, failing to reach me. The monster appeared to be shielded by an invisible force. I could smell its dry dusty odor of a thousand attic corners and the faint metallic scent of old blood underneath it all. Again and again it tried to sink its fangs into my virile body.

A dry chuckle, crisp as dead leaves, shook the hooded figure.

"I told you; in this realm nothing can harm you. Everything is under my control."

"Yeah, okay." I jumped up and dusted myself off. "What else ya got?" I asked.

We walked on.

"Whoa, you got one of those? Cool. I thought for sure those were just made-up fairy tale stuff. Does he have a name?"

"Name? Hmmm, I never thought to ask. Unlike your cartoon or video game versions, this ogre does not talk. He just bashes heads and eats brains."

"Radical."

I had always wondered how brains tasted. Brussels sprouts looked like alien brains but I was disappointed when they tasted like rotten celery. Still, I'd be up for trying brains, especially monkey brains. One time I watched a movie where the foreign royals ate Bonobo brains. It'd be cool if they tasted like sausage or cherry JellO. I was just about to ask when I saw my hooded friend had drifted on ahead of me.

"Hey," I wanted to yell out his name, but I didn't know it. "Hey, hey you, what do they call you?"

He turned in my direction and a chill ran down my spine. My foot faltered on a rock. I picked it up and threw it at the ogre who menaced behind my nameless guide. The rock passed through the invisible barrier into the chamber. It struck the ogre between the eyes, he gave a pissed-off roar, and charged. I stood my ground, another rock in hand, just in case. But like the spider, he couldn't touch me. The barrier was like two-way glass, so to speak, only letting things into the cell, not out.

I threw the other rock. The sound was wet and gooshy as it tore his eye socket. The creepy feeling drained from my body and I felt better. I felt good. Nothing could get me.

I jogged up the dark path.

"So um, this is cool and all. I dig all the creatures, but what am I doing here?" I asked.

He didn't answer but gestured toward another indistinct cell. The darkness was denser, thicker, like sub-oceans under so much pressure the resident animals are deformed and nightmarish. This darkness was like that: compressed compacted night. Yet, I caught the outline of figures crammed against one another slipping and crushing, grinding against distorted edges.

A low rumbling moan, barely audible, like blood rushing through ears after a long run, rolled toward us. It expanded, snaked and climbed until it was a thundering tsunami of misery. The sound wave struck my body and shook loose an old memory.

I had received a high powered magnifying glass for my sixth birthday. It was a present from my dad. It was the last time I saw him.

"If you ever get stranded in the forest or a desert island, you can start a fire when the sun is high and bright. All you need is some dry leaves or twigs," he said. I couldn't wait to try it.

Aunt Gerty chirped in. "Edward." That was my father's name too, but nobody called him that, they all called him Fast Eddy. I was proud to have my father's name. He was a tough guy. Nobody took nothing from Fast Eddy and if he didn't like you...even at six I knew you'd better stay out of his way.

Only, now that I think of it, my ma didn't always stay out of his way. But my old Aunt Gerty, on my mom's side, my great, she went on about the magnifying glass.

"You want him to start a fire, burn down the whole neighborhood? What kind of thing is that to give to a six-year-old? It's not a proper toy. Wouldn't you like a nice little hamster or some Lincoln Logs, honey?"

"Aw, can it, Gertrude. Little Eddy's gotta learn some survival skills. It's a tough world out there and none of us are gonna live forever."

That was the first time I got the creeping crud feeling. The room closed in. My ears filled with cotton. My hands started to sweat. I could no longer focus on the grown-ups arguing.

Did that mean I would die someday?

Surely it didn't.

I was a strong healthy kid, big for my age. I would live forever and so would my dad and my ma — only, they didn't.

I ran outside with my fire-starter and trained it on some dry leaves. An army ant the length of an eyelash came looking for food. I shined the beam of focused sun onto his back and dang if he didn't start smoking. It took a few seconds but he burned and burned, still crawling with his back on fire.

I imagined a tiny voice screeching and screaming. I fried ant after ant that day. The creeping crud went away; my ears returned to normal and the fear turned to elation.

※ ※ ※

I wondered if I had a sound magnifier if I might've heard a moan like the one in the chamber. The dark wall of moaning didn't faze me one bit. Was that all that was hiding in here?

We walked for what seemed hours or minutes or seconds; it was hard to tell. He showed me monsters from fables, from mythology, from horror movies. I saw so many nightmares I couldn't keep them sorted in my crowded mind. Some of them blended into weird amalgamations of each other.

Gnawing maggots ripped at decaying meat. Minotaurs larger than I had imagined. Fire-breathing dragons that smelled of sulfur and barbecue. Vampires, trolls, gryphons, three-headed hounds, lumpy sharp-toothed goblins and birds of prey with beautiful faces that morphed into witchy old ladies.

"Cool vulture chicks," I said.

"They are not *vulture chicks*. They are the forgotten Harpies from times of old."

"Yeah, okay. So this is cool and all, and I appreciate the tour, but, yeah, I'm ready to go."

"Hmmm," was all he said.

I was starting to get kinda irritated and kinda hungry and kinda something else I couldn't put a name to when we stopped at another cell.

I took a deep breath, folded my arms, rolled my eyes and sighed.

"And what's in this one?"

"Look," he replied.

I turned and saw my own reflection.

"What the..." I started to say. I grabbed for his arm, but found myself spun around, no longer looking at my reflection but staring into a shadowed bony face. I was dizzy.

The creeping crud feeling was back. It shook my whole body. The back of my neck was damp. My stomach gurgled, making my mouth water with acidic saliva.

I must be dreaming. Yeah, that's it, this is a dream. I slowed my heart and laughed at myself. Now, to wake up. I pinched myself only to feel a sharp pain in my right thigh. This was no dream.

"What is this?" I rubbed my sweaty hands on my jeans. "This is a joke, right?"

"No joke. Consider it—an invitation."

I calmed a degree.

"Well, thanks but no thanks. As cool as this joint is, I, I don't belong here," I said as calmly as I could.

"Don't you?"

"Noooooo!" I howled. My heart was in my throat. Sweat trickled down my back. Waves of shivers rolled through my body. There must be a way out. This wasn't right. The air became too thin, not enough oxygen for my lungs. I had to get out.

I balled my hands into fists. Kicked at the floor, hoping to find a rock or stick, a weapon I could use. I lunged at the hooded figure, and bounced back like a fly hitting a window. My forearms stung from the impact. My ass hurt where I crashed to the ground. The darkness became richer, swimming through liquid onyx. I had to get out.

"I'm not a nightmare. I'm not an evil man. I'm not even a man yet," I begged.

A low chuckle shimmered his cloak.

"It's not what you are—yet. It's what you will become. Man. The scariest, vilest, cruelest of any creature to exist in the universe."

"But, but, I'm still young, I could change," I whispered.

"Mmmm," he replied with a cold smirk, "and who says I want that?"

8. M IS FOR MOTHER

I threw the baby across the room. It slid down the wall and landed on a shelf of Legos and plastic fruit. *Mama, mama, mama* it echoed an eerie cadence.

"Ah, excuse me mizz. Are you okay?" A middle-aged Hispanic janitor poked his head into my room. "I thought I hear something."

"Uh, no. The toys were stacked too high and one fell." I lied. "Do you happen to have a mini Phillips? I need to pull the battery out of it."

Mama, mama, mama, the toy repeated in a child's voice. I didn't know why it bugged me so much. I liked kids and all the noise that went with them. I wanted kids someday and had already fallen in love with a couple of them. I would scoop up sweet Araceli with her dark hair and light eyes, or Hector with his dimpled smile, in a hot second. I'd quickly grown attached to them.

But, it had been a rough day. My first real teaching assignment turned out to be more challenging than I'd anticipated.

Mama, mama, mama. I'd ignored the damn thing when I sorted the kids for bus and carpool, but with the school empty, in the quiet classroom, it drove me nuts. All morning too, through the pledge, announcements and breakfast, twenty-three minutes of *Mama, mama, mama.*

"Oh, sorry mizz, I don't have no tools on me. I'll bring tomorrow, but it will stop," he looked at his watch, "in about eleven minutes. It talks every day at this time." He continued to peer into the room without stepping inside. "It talks in the morning too."

"Yes, it did. Weird."

"Yes mizz."

"Well it must have something to do with the moisture, don't you think? This classroom's so cold. Look at the condensation on the windows. I once had this singing cactus that would croon *Happy Trails* anytime it rained or I boiled potatoes. The moisture completed the circuit. That's probably it, don't you think?"

Mama, mama, mama droned in the background.

"Yes mizz, that's prob'ly what it is." He left me with the crying doll and my chattering teeth. I'd forgotten to ask about fixing the air-conditioning.

※ ※ ※

The crying doll became part of our routine, a litany in the background of our morning, a closing prayer in the afternoon. The kids named the doll Aiden. I asked them why they chose a boy name for a girl doll and they said, "because that's its name."

My new space heater turned the room into a tropical temperate zone; a monsoon threatened hourly. At least I wasn't shivering when I read *Goodnight Moon*.

"Knock, knock." Kelly Anderson, another first year, (Second grade, I was Kinder), stopped by. "I'm running over to Madeline's Bakery for sandwiches. It's our week for a long lunch. Would you like to go?"

"Sure. Thanks Kelly. Come on in, give me a minute."

"No offense, but your classroom smells funny and creeps me out." She edged inside but stayed near the door.

"Oh, well between the frigid air conditioning, the space-heater's hot air and my runny nose, I can't smell a thing. Maybe there's mold?"

"Maybe, or maybe there's a ghost?" She said with obvious delight. I gave her my best skeptic look.

"Give me proof," I said.

"Well, the lunch ladies were talking. They don't know I speak Spanish, but they were talking about you and wondering how long you'll last."

"What?"

"Yeah, said you were the fourth teacher this year."

"Well, yeah, I knew that. The first one had a baby, the second had a chronic illness and the third moved because her husband got a new job."

"Mm-hmm, doesn't that strike you as odd?"

"No. Why should it?"

"Because no one says the real reason they quit. AND the lunch ladies were talking about espectro and fantasma and the voceado muneca."

"Sorry, I don't speak Spanish."

"Espectro, fantasma – ghost? Muneca – doll?

"Oh that's what the little girls are saying. I thought they were talking about the moon and a yak. That makes much more sense."

"Does it really cry every day on cue?" she asked.

"Yes." I shook my head. "It's got to be something internal. I took the batteries out, which were rusted; it could mean the wiring's gone wonky."

"Oookay. If you say so. Why don't you just get rid of it?"

"I tried. I put it in my car to take to Goodwill, but the kids were so distraught that baby Aiden was gone; I had three girls in tears. I brought it back."

"You do know what Aiden means in Spanish don't you?"

"No, what?" I asked.

"Visitor."

I shouldn't have told Jim about the doll and what Kelly said about a ghost. He loves that kind of shit. He watches ghost hunter shows religiously. I always fall asleep, waking when they reveal the evidence. I could not believe my intelligent, good-looking, electrician boyfriend went for it. He must have a nerdy side I hadn't met yet, I thought.

We packed his truck with gear and headed towards coffee and kolaches. My sleepy nerves had started to jump. I didn't know why. Maybe it was Jim's plan? While I gave my room a make-over, he planned on debunking and ghost-hunting.

I unlocked the outside door and immediately grimaced. I'd forgotten, no air-conditioning on weekends. The corridor was stuffy and heavy as we slogged down the hall. I struggled with the key, balancing my box against the wall. Jim, being the gentleman, set down his equipment and helped me.

Cold air surged into the hall, curled around, and beckoned us in. We gladly stepped into my cool classroom and turned on the lights.

"Whoa, Kelly was right, this joint does smells funky. Brrrrr, you know ghosts like cold," Jim said.

I held my tongue and kept from rolling my eyes. Instead I leaned over and kissed him. He smelled good. Clean. He kissed me back and leaned me against the door jam. I smiled under his lips and slipped out the side.

"Ever do it in a school?" He waggled his eyebrows.

"Uh, no, and I'm not doing it today."

"Come on." He playfully grabbed my belt loops and pulled me towards him. "Nobody's here." I sighed and made a face.

"Okay Ms. Branson. But if I'm a really bad boy will you spank me?" I threw my new curtains at him and went to work. At least he dispelled my unease about the ghost hunting.

I pulled down the old bulletin board graphics. The empty spots left dark silhouettes in weird shapes from where the sun never hit. It gave me a great idea for an art project with the kids. I filed it away in the back of my mind.

"So when does this phenomenon with the doll happen?" Jim asked.

I looked up at the classroom clock.

"Oooo, in about four minutes. 8:05, every day."

Sure enough, I had just finished pulling down the ancient, dusty curtains and away she cried. *Mama, mama, mama.*

"Ohhhh babe, can you hit record on the DVD recorder." He was thrilled. I obliged. Suddenly, the fire-truck flashed its red light and the retro robot I'd purchased for my new theme began marching in the box. This was different. I prickled and felt off-kilter, almost dizzy. Jim started talking to the air.

"Is there someone here who would like to talk to us?"

"Jim, you sound ridiculous," I joked.

"Shhhh, this is how the pros do it." He winked. "Would you like to tell us something? One cry, for yes, two cries for no." The doll continued her rhythmic wail. I strode to the fire truck, determined to find the logical cause of its flashing.

"No, don't do that."

"I'm just checking it." I scowled. I switched the on/off back and forth. Nothing happened, the light continued to flash weakly in the morning sun, but I had to admit to myself, it was getting weird. "Um, do you think it feels colder in here than when we came in?"

"Shhhh please, I'm recording." He sounded so earnest.

"What? A baby doll?" I whispered.

"EVPs. You remember from the show, electronic voice phenomenon."

"Ohhhh, right, later when you review the audio you'll hear answers to your questions." I humored him and quietly continued to work while he asked the uninvited questions with no responses. At exactly 8:28 the doll stopped and the truck and robot stilled.

"Whoa, that was sooo cool!" Jim twirled me around, kissed me and rushed to his camcorder. "Let's see if we got anything on this baby."

He looked like a kid opening the biggest present at his birthday. I watched his handsome face and thought what cute babies he'd make. Maybe the classroom wasn't such a bad place to do it. I laughed to myself and went back to my curtains. After a bit, he clicked off the camcorder and sighed.

"Well?" I asked.

"Nothing." He pouted. "Come on. You were here. You

saw it. You heard it. It was too bright to get the fire truck but I did get the *Mamas*, on tape."

"Any EVPs?" I raised my eyebrows.

"No." He looked around. "Does it feel warmer in here, now?"

"Sure, it always takes a while for the space heater to warm up."

"Kate, you didn't turn the heater on. Look."

He was right, but the morning was sunny and with the curtains off the windows, it was bound to warm up. I continued to spruce up my room and pushed my uneasy feeling away, ignoring the warning in my gut.

Jim took apart every toy with batteries and switches and tested them with his voltage meter, often yelling out, "dead, live, live, dead." He also dismantled the talking books, which occasionally gave spontaneous recitations. He even tried to trace the electrical wiring to the thermostat, but found the walls were poured concrete, electrical wires embedded.

By the time I sorted through the stacks of leftover teaching crap, I was ready to tackle the book shelves and corner cabinets. As soon as we pulled the shelf away, a putrid smell consumed the room. We had to run into the hall to catch our breath.

"What the hell?" Jim asked. "When was this school built?"

"Uh, in the fifties I think. Why?"

"Well, maybe it was built on a dump or swamp or natural drainage area?"

"Nope. Kelly and I were just talking about this at lunch."

"About the funky smell?"

"No, about the trees."

"What about them?"

"That we have such nice mature old oak trees and she said this used to be immigrant cottages. They kept as many trees as they could, I guess."

"Huh, well that doesn't account for the odd smell."

I shrugged. We held our breath and inspected. No sign of mold or broken pipes. A faint brown stain smudged the wall, like spilled coffee on linen. I grabbed the bleach-water and sprayed the wall. Then we dashed back to the hall for another gulp of air.

"Let's move the big wood cabinets then break for lunch. Whaddaya say?" I wheezed.

"You're the boss." We inched the heavy cabinet away from the wall. Same weird stain, same weird smell. Rinse, lather, repeat. By the fifth run we were tired and giddy, hands on each other's shoulders.

When we left for lunch I promised Jim when we came back we could stay until dark. I should've locked the door.

We returned and found the cabinets had been moved back and the room straightened. My stomach twisted, but then I thought, it must have been the custodians, which made me feel worse. I didn't wanted them to think it was their job to fix my mess. Tears came to my eyes before I could stop them.

"What's the matter, Babe?"

"I don't know. I just got this deep wave of sadness, like I lost something very important. It's probably exhaustion. It's been a tough week."

"Maybe. Are you sure you're okay?" I scrunched my face and wiped my eyes. Jim gave me a sweet hug. The melancholy passed but niggled my nerves. I couldn't settle down. I put my jangly energy to use and continued to sort through cabinets and boxes.

Jim lugged my castoffs to the trash. I focused on finishing my mid-century vintage vision for the room. The classroom transformed into an artsy cool learning environment, no penguins, no monkeys, no ladybugs, one hundred percent original and all me. Happy warmth spread across my insides. I smiled.

"It looks wonderful, Kate. I wish I could go to school here." He gave me a chaste hug, but I grabbed him and gave him a big kiss. I was so overwhelmed with joy, tears rushed to my eyes again. Conflicting emotions tugged at my center.

"What's wrong?" Jim felt the wet on my cheeks, the change in my lips.

"I don't know." My heart fell to my knees and the strange melancholy returned.

Suddenly, we were plunged into darkness. The baby doll cried, *Mama, mama, mama.* The red fire truck light ricocheted off the dark walls and gave the room a disturbing glow.

"Mama, mama, mama, ayudame Aida, Mama, mama, mama, ayudame Aida."

Oh my god, I thought, the doll, just talked. The doll just talked. Tears streamed from my eyes. The hairs on my arms stood up. I could not believe what was happening. Jim's handsome face distorted in the flashing light. He rubbed my arms. I steepled my hands in front of my lips, blowing hot air to keep myself from hyperventilating.

"You okay?" Jim whispered; he was unmistakably excited. "I'm going to go turn on the camcorder." He squeezed my hand. "Are you okay with that?"

Part of me wanted him to stay planted by my side. Part of me wanted to run out the door and never come back. But the teacher part of me, my logic side, wanted proof that it really was happening.

"I'm okay," I rasped. Jim hastened to the recorder.

"Mama mama ayudame Aida." The voice no longer sounded electronic, it sounded like a small frightened child. A chill ran up my spine. Jim sidled back to me.

"What is…" I began. He cut me off with a finger to his lips and directed me to the opposite corner of the room. I was cold and hot at the same time. His arms felt comforting but not enough. My eyes continued to leak.

"Jim, what is it saying? Eye – you – da? Is it I, you, dad? I, you, dada?"

"Mama, mama, mama, ayudame Aida, mama, mama,

mama." We strained our ears. Then we heard it. A sweet lullaby, not from the doll, but dulcet tones emanating from the stained walls.

> *Besitos de Chocolate*
> *besitos de rica miel*
> *besitos de cacahuate*
> *rellenos de fresa y nuez*
>
> *Si quieres unos besitos*
> *sabrosos yo te daré*
> *tu dime de que los quieres*
> *y pronto te besaré*
>
> *Yo tengo un surtido rico*
> *de fresa, vainilla y nuez*
> *mis más exquisitos besos*
> *con gusto yo te daré*

I flapped my hands and ran them over my face. Jim grabbed them and held them in his. We looked into each other's eyes.

"Spanish," we murmured. Jim was way ahead of me and he pulled out his phone. The screen light washed his face in eerie shadows. He tried a couple of spellings until he got it: Ayudame—Help me.

I trembled. My mouth went dry. The ghost child cried *mama, help me, Aida.* My heart lurched. I wanted to reach into the void, the dark, wherever the lost soul was. I wept more. Jim pulled me close.

"What about the song?" I asked softly.

"I don't know. It's too muted but it will be on the recording. We can boost the volume and look it up later."

Jim guided me down to a sitting position and we sat like puppets. My fingers twined in his, hands in his lap with my head on his shoulder. I gently cried, not knowing why.

What seemed like hours later, the room quieted and the lights snapped back on. I became self-conscious of how blotchy my face looked. Jim read my mind and stroked my hairline.

"Compassion is beautiful on you, babe."

I smiled. I wanted to marry that man. But first things first, we needed to check the evidence.

※ ※ ※

The next night at home we watched the video, mesmerized by the dark form we hadn't seen in the classroom. Jim adjusted the contrast. A shadowy man darted from side to side, raising his hands over his head and lowering them repeatedly. We thought there may have been another figure, but couldn't be sure. We invited Kelly over as our official translator and she decoded the song:

Chocolate kisses
rich honey kisses
peanut kisses
strawberry and walnut stuffings

If you want some kisses
I will give you delicious
you tell me that you love me
and soon I'll kiss

I have a rich variety
strawberry, vanilla and walnut
my most delicious kisses
I gladly give

We did some digging, ghost-hunter style. The Post Register had a Way-back Archive and for $7.99 a month or $4.95 for a day, we could search the entries. We chose the day pass and found two-thousand, seven hundred and fifty two articles about murder, but when we put in the name Aida and murder we only got three.

Oct. 6th, 1948
Jose Munoz seemed like a regular guy. He worked on the Liverwood farm as a ranch hand and translator for migrant workers. Neighbors described him as helpful and courteous. "Always kept the place nice and neat, a good neighbor except when he had one of those spells." At approximately 8:05am Munoz had *one of his spells*. When it was over, three people were dead, bludgeoned to death with a hammer. Fingerprints found on the hammer link Munoz to the crime as well

as eye-witness reports of yelling coming from the home, according to police reports. The victims were illegal immigrants Araceli Gonzales, twenty-three years in age, and her sister Guadalupe Gonzales, twenty, and her son Aiden Reyes, five. Still missing is a five-year-old female, Aida Munoz, who may have witnessed the crime. If you see this child, please alert authorities. She may be very frightened and does not speak good English. Munoz is still at large and is believed to be armed and dangerous. If you have any information regarding this crime, please notify your local authorities. This brutal murder is one of the worst tragedies in county history.

We sat back in stunned silence.

"That has to be our Aida," I said.

"What? I thought the doll's name was Aiden? Why would it call Aida?" Kelly squawked.

"Read the report again. The other child, the five-year-old boy named Aiden, was killed. He's calling for his cousin, Aida. I think," Jim answered.

"Ohhh, okay." She gnawed her fingernails and walked in a circle. "Wait, wait, wait. Twenty-three!"

"What?" I asked.

"Don't you get it?" Jim and I gave her blank looks.

"Twenty-three, the mom, of the girl they never found, Araceli Gonzales, was twenty-three when she died. The doll cries for exactly twenty-three minutes!"

"Is there more than one ghost?" I asked.

"I don't know, but I think so," Jim answered. "We've got three who died a violent death and one who was never found. Didn't you say the kids named the doll Aiden?"

"Yes," I answered. It started to make some kind of horrible sense. My skin became gooseflesh, simultaneously cold and hot again and my eyes filled with tears but didn't spill. I read the article again.

"Did you note the time? 8:05. That's the time it starts every morning," I said. I didn't believe it. I didn't want to believe any of it was true. Real ghosts had a much bigger implication than I wanted to deal with.

I focused on the tangible. I did the math in my head.

"If Aida were still alive she'd be fifty-five."

❉ ❉ ❉

After exhaustive internet searches and embarrassing phone calls, we found our Aida in San Antonio. We drove down there with our story and video and set up camp at a nearby hotel. Even with Kelly translating and explaining about the *muneca* and lullaby, she declined. We couldn't convince her to watch the video or come back with us.

Aida said she needed to stay in San Antonio in case her wayward daughter came home. It had been five years since her daughter had disappeared, taking Aida's grandbaby with her. No, she would not leave. She wouldn't go back to the evil place, even if they'd built a school over it.

By the time we convinced Aida to watch the video footage, we were out of money and time. It was hearing the lullaby on tape that finally convinced her to come back with us.

※ ※ ※

Back in my classroom Aida stared at the darkest corner. I sat between Kelly and Jim. Even though Aida spoke adequate English, she was more comfortable with Spanish. Plus, after dragging Kelly to San Antonio, there was no way she was going to miss it.

Minutes stretched for hours. My skin prickled in waves upon my body. My eyes swam with extra moisture, yet my mouth was dry. Kelly and Jim vibrated with excitement.

"Mama, mama, mama."

It began. The fire truck flashed its red light. Aida looked at us and truly believed for the first time. She grabbed Kelly's hand and held it tight.

"Estas bien?' Kelly asked.

"Si. I no really believe it," Aida said in her thick Spanish accent. She made the sign of the cross and kissed the one at the end of her necklace.

"Mama, mama, mama, ayuda, mama."

Aida inhaled sharply. Her face displayed conflicting emotions, distorted as it was by the flashing red light. She squirmed in her seat and looked around, but before she had a chance to flee, we heard the faint melody of the lullaby.

Besitos de Chocolate
besitos de rica miel
besitos de cacahuate
rellenos de fresa y nuez

Aida accompanied the unseen vocalist on the second verse. The living and ghost mother's voices blended in achingly beautiful harmony. I shivered.

"Aida, Aida, mi bebe," the ghost voice whispered.

"Aida, Aida, my baby," Kelly leaned over and translated. Her words stuttered in my ear as she quivered beside me.

I held Jim tighter and whispered to him. "Is it Aida's mother we hear?"

"Yes I think that's who's singing."

We tried to comprehend what was happening. The grown woman who sat next to us, Aida, spoke with the ghost.

"Si Mama, es mio."

(Yes, mama it's me)

"Te escaparse?" the ghost asked.

(You escaped?) The translation came smoother and faster. We no longer heard the Spanish tongue.

"Yes, Mama, I ran and ran all the way to Gemma's. I hid for days in her closet." Aida gulped for air. "I did not know if you were dead, or little Aiden, or Aunt Lupe. I was a coward."

"No baby, no. You did good. You could not save us." Aida's body shook with sobs. We added ours as hot tears rolled down our cheeks.

"All these years I thought, maybe if I had stayed, I could have saved you, Mama."

"No mi hija, no. You lived and gave me grandbabies. Araceli, my namesake, looks just like you did at her age," said the ghost.

"What do you mean? How do you know your great-granddaughter?" Aida asked.

"She es aqui. I have seen her. She is beautiful and muy inteligente. I remember what your sweet face looked like when you were five. Now I see you as a beautiful abuelita. It makes me happy." The ghost of Araceli Gonzales began to fade, her voice turned to a whisper.

"Mama, don't go," Aida cried.

"Mi hija. I have seen my baby girl grown and brought you together with your granddaughter. I can go in peace."

"Mama," Aida wept.

"Te amo chula. It will be many years before I see you again. Live well." She faded away, the light stopped flashing and a fresh scent, which hadn't been there before, filled the classroom.

It all made sense: The pretty little girl with the curly black hair and gray eyes, Araceli Sanchez, was in my class. She was Aida's granddaughter, great-granddaughter of the ghost, Araceli Gonzales, her namesake, killed fifty years ago on this spot.

The doll had begun its litany with this year's crop of Kinders. And oh, yes, Araceli and Aida had the same gray eyes.

9. THE OAKEN

*T*he first tribes of man were led by three brothers. It had been foretold that when first man is in need, a magician will appear and grant the worthy one wish each. That time had come. The three brothers journeyed across barren lands and passed packs of lean wolves grown mean in their struggle. Love and understanding between their races long ago lost.

They reached the onyx mountain. Bodies bloodied from climbing on sharp edges, they found the hidden entrance.

The youngest of the three brothers, who had been scarred by fire, approached the magician.

"What is it you wish?" the magician asked.

"I wish to have beauty that inspires my people and doesn't turn children away."

"It shall be done."

The middle brother, the weakest and smallest of the three, approached.

"And what is your wish?"

"I wish to have strength and armor to protect myself and my people from enemies."

"It shall be done."

The oldest brother, handsome and strong, unburdened with insecurities, asked only for long life and the ability to provide for his people.

"It shall be done. Return to your villages. Rise at midnight on the first black moon, mix this powder with water and drink. As the morning sun rises, so shall your wishes be granted."

They returned to their villages.

The white eye of the night sky grew smaller until the moon goddess slept. They followed the magician's instructions.

Morning greeted the youngest brother transformed into delicate blue flowers. He lay across the flat expanse of land surrounding his village. When his people awoke, they ran through his fields of blue, awed and inspired by his beauty. So Bluebonnets came into the world.

As the sun came upon the second brother, it glinted off his tough accordion hide. He became strong and impregnable. So Armadillos came into the world.

Daybreak found the eldest brother's arms turned to branches, his torso a strong trunk, his legs and feet sturdy roots. In the oldest recorded language his name is known as Eiche, Aik, or Oak. His acorns nourished his people. His branches provided shade and beauty. His severed limbs became huts and boats. He stayed green and steady even in the deepest of

winters. His Oaklets spread far and wide across the south of his lands. So
Live Oak came into the world.

The boys lounged in the semi-cool under the wide porch. This summer found them retreating to their subterranean lair more often, even inviting the girls. The severe drought had prevented the usual weeds and dampness, allowing them to build a fort under the ancient porch. Light beams streamed like spotlights from drain holes drilled into the wooden deck. The shafts of light illuminated a collection of cars, robots and one treasured stuffed animal. Almost too old for such toys, the adolescents clung to their childhood like icing on an uncooled cake.

"So, are y'all gonna come with us to the cemetery tonight?" Camellia asked. Linden ignored her as he twisted the robot into standing position. "Well, are you?" She grabbed her stuffed rabbit and fretted its long ears in a knot.

"We've gone four nights now and nothing's happened," he replied.

"Yeah, all we do is sit under the big oak and play truth-or-dare. I'm sick of you girls trying to trick us into kissing you," Buckie said.

"I'm, well, I, I, I'm..." she said, her blush undetectable in the dusk of their fortress. "Th, th, that's beside the point. Tonight will be different. Jujuba, Holly's guinea pig died, and we're gonna bury it tonight."

"I don't know how you're going to get it in the ground. That dirt is hard-packed." Linden polished the metal robot and placed it back in the spotlight. "You'd think they'd have a watering system at the graveyard, at least all the trees there aren't dead," he said.

"Yeah, I know. Did you hear about the oak that fell into Mr. Bladdernut's class when he was setting up? It crashed through the window, spraying glass everywhere," Buckie hooted. "Man, I wish I would have been there."

"Don't rush it. We've only got a week left of summer. Besides, you wouldn't be in his class anyway, you're not advanced," Cam teased.

"Neither are you," Buckie teased back.

"Math isn't my thing. I'm in advanced English. Burch's summer folktale assignment was easy for me. I read a lot of interesting stories. Anyway, that's how I found out about you-know-what."

❋ ❋ ❋

Old Lady Dahoon had a shrunken apple head. Her skin folded like leather waves upon her dark face, her onyx eyes twinkled.

"I know why you've come," she said.

Camellia shivered. Sweat broke across her back. The scent of ivory soap and dust caught in her nose. She balled her fists, quelled her fear and closed her eyes. She said a quick prayer hoping Jesus would forgive her and understand, it was nothing against Him.

"You know why I'm here?"

"I've written it down for you, dearie. Take this. Come back and see me if it doesn't work. It's been a long time."

Cam stretched her trembling hand toward the tiny figure. The brown hand shot out faster than would have been expected for a lady her age. It was hot, almost to the point of uncomfortable, like a bad sunburn. Cam fought the urge to pull back. The crone forced the parchment paper into Cam's young, cool hand. Camellia Cottonwood ran all the way home, scared, exhilarated, but most of all, hopeful.

※ ※ ※

"But we haven't seen anything, have we?" Linden said.

"I know, but the old stories said….and I'm following Old Dahoon's instructions. Buckie, think of your daddy's farm," Camellia said. "Think of the whole county."

Buckie fought an urge to shiver. He wasn't a titty-baby, but this stuff was weird. Girls. The only reason he went to the cemetery was for Cam. Even though he teased her about truth-or-dare, he liked kissing her. It was like a new flavor of ice cream he couldn't describe. He felt full and slightly altered.

"Yeah well, anyway," Buckie snickered, "I heard old Bladdernut broke his arm when he fell, running for the door." They all laughed.

"So, where's Holly, anyway," Linden asked.

"Her mama made her come right home after summer

school. She's gonna get Jujuba and bring her...."

"Linden. Camellia. Buckeye. Come out from under there. How many times I got to tell you? Y'all too old to be playing like little Maggie. Come on, your mamas'll be wondering where you got off to."

"Magnolia's not down here," Linden replied.

"Well, go on and check the coop and bring her on in for a wash. Make sure they got enough water. Lord knows I don't need chickens dying. It's bad enough we lost the milk goat."

"Yes ma'am." They scrambled out into the fading light.

A sliver of the moon hung in the pitch of night. The kids traipsed along in companionable silence. Boy Scout flashlights led the way, their glow casting eerie shadows where they slid between tombstones, creating figures where none should be.

It was easy enough to sneak out. Since the beginning of summer they'd been bunking on sleeping porches. Linden had it the hardest, his on the second floor, but he was an expert climber and siblings Maggie and Philbert slept like the dead.

They arrived at the biggest tree in the graveyard. It swayed rhythmically, like a breathing man. Buckie shook the heebie jeebies off his back. It's all nonsense anyhow, he thought. How could they solve the drought when the scientists and meteorologists couldn't? Old Lady Dahoon didn't say anything about a tree, but Cam insisted on the location. She'd read many stories which included trees.

"Linden, I need your flashlight on me, not on the branches," Cam said.

"I thought I heard something. Maybe an owl or a raccoon," Linden replied.

"You know we haven't seen any critters since the end of May. Holly, bring your guinea pig, Jujuba, over here, please," Cam continued.

The five kids gathered closer at the base of the tree where gnarled roots bulged like arthritic hands. Chubby Myrtle sat down and pulled a Squirrel Nut Zipper from her pocket.

"Myrtle, how many times do I hafta tell you, if you're gonna bring something to eat, you gotta bring enough for everyone," Holly chided.

"Can we get on with this? Buckie, you got the watering can? Linden, shine your light along the roots. I thought I saw a crevice in the dirt." He flicked his flashlight along the fingered corms. "Just there. Yeah, that'll do," Cam said.

They dampened the earth and widened the crack with a hand spade and pocket knife. They were all supposed to bring something to dig with, but only Cam complied. Buckie always carried his knife. They worked the moist dirt wide enough to fit the cigar box containing Jujuba's remains.

"Everybody add your object. The directions said something of value from each of us. Holly you're already giving Jujuba." A hot tear trickled down Holly's cheek, unseen in the dark.

"Oh no. I forgot. I don't have anything," Myrtle whined.

"Looks like you'll hafta put in your nut bar," Linden snorted.

"Aww, but can't I just have one bite?"

"No, I think it's better in the wrapper. Hand it over."

Myrtle reluctantly handed Cam her treat. Linden forked over his favorite miniature cap gun. Buckie closed his pocket knife and handed it to Cam. I'll come back for it later, he thought. The sooner they finished this weirdness, the sooner they could play truth-or-dare. Heat rushed to his face and tingled his stomach at the thought. Cam took the locket from around her neck, sighed and placed it in the box.

"Do you have the pin?" Holly smudged a tear from her face and dug in her pocket.

"Do we have to do it again? I'm running out of fingers," she complained.

Cam removed the needle from the small tin box. Everyone except Myrtle held out their pinkie. Holly grabbed Myrtle's hand, Cam pricked and squeezed before she could protest. Myrtle slumped back to her perch and loudly nursed her finger. Once everyone had dribbled their blood over Jujuba's body, Cam slid the box into the hole and filled it with dirt.

"Aren't you gonna say the thingy, you know, on the paper," Buckie asked.

Cam had it memorized the first day but continued to hold the incantation script in her hand each night in case she forgot; she never did. Tonight, she was weary.

The summer quest had uncovered varied folktales: Indians talking to tree spirits, ancient Greeks calling on the dead, druids beseeching rain gods. Her mind went into overdrive wondering if they could do something similar. She wasn't any of those, but she knew where she could find an Indian. She didn't think Jesus would mind. She hoped Old Dahoon would help her and thought she had; now she wasn't so sure.

"Can it be someone else's turn?" she asked.

No one volunteered. Linden kicked the dirt, Buckie fiddled with his flashlight, Holly crossed her fingers and said a prayer, Myrtle continued to suck her finger.

"Oh, jeeze, I'll do it," Buckie said. "Here, you hold the flashlight Cam, give me the paper." They awkwardly exchanged items and flushed at the touch of skin.

"Ahem, Earth Mother we, uh, donate our life and uh, energy so you may bless us with nourishing rain and abundant crops. Amen."

"You don't need to say amen," Cam whispered.

"Yeah, um, NOT amen."

They took a collective breath as a breeze blew Cam's hair. It tickled her cheek and the earth vibrated under their feet.

"Do you feel that?" Holly murmured.

They inched closer, grabbing each other's hands. The wind blew stronger, tugging at Holly's skirt, flapping Linden's collar. Flashlights flickered out. Buckie and Linden dropped the girls' hands and furiously banged on their useless lights. Myrtle screamed and jumped from her perch, running to Holly and Cam. The wind whipped hair and clothes. Dust powdered their bodies. A faint light radiated from the fissure. Myrtle emitted a long high-pitched scream. Her finger pointed toward the glow.

Suddenly everything went black. No wind. No light. No sound. Before they could take another breath, flashlights flickered back to life, the earth stilled.

"Whoa. What was that?" Linden was the first to break the silence.

Cam released her grip on Buckie. "We did it," she said.

"Uh, what exactly did we do?" Holly asked.

"I...I don't know, but something happened. I've got to go back to Dahoon."

"She creeps me out. Do you think she's a witch?" Holly asked.

"There aren't any real witches, are there?"

❀ ❀ ❀

They lounged in the semi-cool under the wide porch. Sun blistered the afternoon and faded the night's terrors. Their fears seemed childish and silly in the light of day.

"Thanks for meeting me again everybody. Did y'all bring acorns from the dead trees?" Cam asked.

"Yeah, I found an uneaten squirrel stash. Here," Buckie said. The other kids deposited their offerings into Cam's faded feed sack.

"What are you gonna do with them all?"

"You'll see."

※ ※ ※

Under a dark moon, the gang re-assembled beneath the great Live Oak. The air was infused with cool moisture. Bare arms prickled at the chill. For the first time in a long time, Holly shivered. Cam shifted her knapsack and pulled out five tan muffins, still warm from the evening's baking. She handed them round, steam rose from each.

"So, what are these?" Linden asked.

"Oh, I get it, that's what you did with the acorns," Holly answered.

"Yes. We eat the acorn muffins. Then, we see," Cam said.

"I'm not eating it. I'm allergic to nuts."

"Myrtle you are NOT allergic to nuts. Squirrel Nut Zipper bar?"

"Oh, do you think it's still good?" She glanced at last night's dirt mound, her stomach growled.

Little did she know her snack was gone. After walking Cam home, Buckie returned, retrieved his knife and ate Myrtle's candy. He took no notice of the newly emerged blue flowers at the gravesite.

They ate the acorn bread in silence. It was tastier than expected.

"Does anyone feel anything? See anything?" Cam asked. All heads shook no.

"Linden, stop doing that with your flashlight in the branches." Buckie looked up.

"I'm not doing anything. My flashlight's pointing down." Four sets of eyes slowly followed Buckie's line of vision.

Filmy mists swirled around the tree-top, spiraling in and out of branches like otters. Camellia shivered involuntarily, physically shaking, and moved to Buckie's side. He swallowed hard and gritted his teeth. Cam's presence felt solid and real. He couldn't reconcile the incongruity of what he saw.

Holly and Myrtle on either side of Linden clung to him and buried their heads in his chest. He draped his arms over them protectively.

The mists circled closer, lower and lower as the ground roiled below their feet. The kids stood like stone pillars while the amoebic forms took human shapes. Shear cloth draped skeletal frames. Garbed in a flowing gown, a female figure descended and hovered in front of Cam and Buckie.

"You have been given the gift of sight and we are grateful. We cannot do this alone." The voice sounded everywhere and nowhere at once, like it came from an empty barn. Buckie's stomach lurched and he had to swallow hard to contain his fear. Tears glistened in Camellia's eyes.

Myrtle whimpered and begged to go home, but didn't take her face from Linden's chest.

Holly bit her lower lip as tears rolled down her cheeks. She was terrified and strangely sad. "Look at them all." She directed their attention to the colonized graveyard. Everywhere they looked, ghostly specters twisted and churned around trees and tombstones.

Camellia took a deep breath and steadied her voice. "What are the red ones?"

"Good. You can see them as well. The vista bread has done its job. You will not have the sight long, but as you can see, we are out-numbered," the ghost lady said.

Buckie, Cam, Lin and Holly stole another glance. They saw the red vapors exceeded the white.

"I don't understand," Holly whispered. The figure floated to face her. The chill turned icy, and only then did Holly feel the wind thrashing against her thin frame. Her heart drummed. Her mouth filled with tinny saliva as she squeezed closer to Linden almost toppling his balance.

"The malignant spirits are stripping the life force from the trees. Have you not noticed your foliage and animals dying? Too many of our brethren have died from this drought. The spirit balance is now bent against us. We Live Oaks are the last stronghold and we are losing. We need new life."

"What can we do?" The wind tore Linden's question from his lips.

"There is one of you who knows."

They looked into each other's eyes searching for answers. Not a single face reflected the knowledge needed.

"I know. I know. I know." A cackling figure sprung from

behind the great trunk.

Cam gasped in recognition.

"You would do this?" The spirit addressed the old crone.

"I am old and close to my time."

"You will be bound with me and the others in the Live Oak."

"Yes," Old Dahoon answered.

The ground shuddered. The wind howled like a tea kettle at first boil, a million tiny pins pricked their skin. The kids staggered and took several steps back as the crevice opened like a wound. Dahoon walked into the dark slit of earth. Camellia wanted to cry *NO*, but the words stuck in her throat. The world throbbed and pitched, heaving the kids to the ground.

Dahoon was gone.

Suddenly everything went black. No wind. No light. No sound. Before they could take another breath, their flashlights flickered back to life and the earth stilled. The kids rose from where they'd fallen and dusted themselves off. They nodded to one another and silently stumbled out of the graveyard, past the railroad tracks towards town.

A dry bush rustled on their left as an armadillo waddled across their path. Cam and Buckie, hand in hand, smiled and knew it was a good sign to see a critter again. They reached the town square in silence. It looked smaller than they'd remembered, or maybe they were bigger.

As they made their way home it began to rain.

10. HAINT BLUE

I woke grasping for air.

My body shook with fear, the blood, water, and throbbing pain still fresh and real. A dim outline of my bedroom window was visible through the early dawn light. I took a deep breath and let it out slowly, just like yoga class. In through the nose, count to ten, out through the mouth, count to ten. The dream faded but the loud thumping continued. I thought maybe someone was knocking on the front door, I hardly knew a soul.

We hadn't lived here long. Harvey had got a job in Austin, but we wanted to try small town living and found a darling little town just twenty-five minutes away. Harvey was convinced it was Mayberry. I was convinced Mayberry didn't exist anymore, but the town was charming and the house was perfect: a beautiful

1907 Edwardian, not quite Victorian or Craftsman, but big and gorgeous with a giant wrap-around porch. It was the house we'd always dreamed of.

I flung myself out of bed and threw on one of my Frida Khalo dresses, a little cotton Mexican dress with embroidered flowers. I traipsed to the front door and found the porch empty. Bang, bang – bang bang bang – bang. I recognized the rhythm as the same from my dream. The sound taunted from the second floor. I grabbed the kitchen broom and headed up.

We'd been told a lot of *critters* liked to make their way up the hollow front porch columns and nest in the attic. Why did this stuff always happen when Harvey wasn't home? Not that I was the squeamish type, but what if it was a bat and it bit me, I went rabid, foamed at the mouth and couldn't drive myself to the hospital? Or what if it was a giant raccoon that went for my throat? I let my imagination reel all possible scenarios before I reigned myself in. I couldn't shake the dream. My heart still pounded.

If only the kids were home. I always slept better when the kids were under the same roof. Harvey thought it would be a great idea for them to visit his parents so I could unpack without constant interruption. I knew he was right. I'm unstoppable when I get going, but my son would have been all over this. Well, at least he would have grabbed his pirate sword and given me some back-up.

I crept up the stairs. A chill ran up my spine. A vague

feeling of deja vu teased at my mind. I gripped my broom tighter.

"Hellloooo, anybody up there?" I said into the murky, refinished attic space.

"Bang, bang – bang bang bang – bang," the house replied.

I made the top landing, turned left and headed for the sound. It was loudest in what was to be my son's room. The door creaked as I eased it open.

I picked my way across the unassembled bunk beds. The sound grew louder as I sidled toward the windows. Bang, bang – bang bang bang – bang. Sweat broke across my back. I slowly raised the curtain, turned my head, dropped the broom, and ran to the other side of the room.

Nothing flew out at me. I wiped my hands over my face and took a deep breath. Bang, bang – bang bang bang – bang. I re-armed and attacked. This time, I flipped up the curtain and tucked it behind the rod.

Nothing. My shoulders relaxed. I laughed at myself and leaned my weapon against the wall. A loosened screen banged against the window. What had I been afraid of? My dream had engendered a fear I couldn't completely divest.

I opened the window and pulled the screen the rest of the way off and set it inside. I crawled out and sat on the roof. The view was beautiful. The morning had a blue haze of soft sapphire. The crisp air chilled my damp skin, but it felt good. This is my house, my new house, I thought. This is the house I will grow old in, maybe die in.

Sage green leaves twinkled against the gnarled oak branches. I loved that they didn't lose their leaves in the winter. Live Oak, that's what they were called. My eyes spied a strange pattern in the other fallen leaves, but before I could think more about it, the doorbell rang.

I almost lost my footing but recovered and bounded down the stairs. Someone had to be there this time. I couldn't imagine the wind could ring a doorbell.

To my surprise our perky real-estate agent smiled at me from behind the wavy glass. Her bleached hair was piled as high as it would go without being a beehive. *The higher the hair, the closer to God*, so they said here.

"Oh, good morning Kristine. Um, hi. Come on in," I said.

"I hope it's not too early. I have a couple of houses to show and wanted to drop off this welcome basket. Sorry I've not been over sooner. Welcome!"

She handed me a large basket filled with *Hill Country* wine, home-made bread, local goat cheese, sausages and something I'd just come to like called Kolaches. Maybe this *was* Mayberry?

"You'll want to put those sausages and cheese in the fridge, darling," she said in her Texas twang.

"Thank you so much. This is really sweet of you."

"Just a big Texas welcome," she replied, her smile lighting up her face and crinkling her eyes.

"Do you have time for a coffee? We can dig into the

Kolaches."

"Oh bless your heart, no. I've got appointments." We moved onto the porch.

"So how do you like the house? I can't say I've ever sold a house that the clients only saw on the internet," she said.

"I can't say we've ever bought a house that way either. We took a leap of faith. I think we were meant to live here. I love it, especially the porch. The pictures just didn't do it justice," I replied.

"I know, isn't it gorgeous? Well I suppose you'll be painting the porch ceiling Haint Blue then?"

"No, I don't think blue is in our color scheme. We were thinking more greens, yellows, maybe a dash of red."

"Oh bless your heart, that's got nothing to do with it. Here in the south it's a bit of a tradition to paint the ceilings of porches a pale shade of blue. It's supposed to keep the hornets away."

I gave her a quizzical look.

"The blue is supposed to look like sky and confuse the wasps and discourage them from making their nests."

"Oh, hmm, that's funny. Well, I might just have to think about that. Thanks for the advice."

"Don't hesitate to call if you need anything or have any questions. You know we're coming up on our Christmas celebrations in the town square. You don't want to miss it. Everyone dresses up Victorian and there are performances and food and craft booths. It's all very festive." She looked up at the sky, shading her eyes.

"I do wish the morning chill would stay so the children could enjoy the hot chocolate though. The afternoon heat is not very Christmassy, but it is good for house sales." She gave me her winning salesman smile and clambered down the stairs.

I stayed on the porch, looked up at the ceiling and tried to picture it blue.

※ ※ ※

The woman in the box looked so young, barely out of girlhood, like a keepsake China doll. Her long honey hair appeared to have been pulled down from an up-do, swirled ringlets still clung to the top of her head. Waves bounded in chaotic rivers around her face. Her dress was full, framed by poufy sleeves and a high collar. I stole looks from the corner of my eye, afraid to make eye-contact. The box was enclosed in clear glass except for the part I was painting.

She was talking and gesturing but I couldn't hear what she was saying. The more I painted the more frantic she became. My hand continued the wide even strokes. Blue paint covered the entire bottom of the box. As I advanced toward the top she rose to her knees. Her hands pressed the top of the box, pounding with her palms. I took my eyes off the paint and glanced her way.

Her blue-green eyes locked on mine.

The world tilted and shifted. I was in the box. I was pounding on the top. A dark figure was painting me in. Water from an invisible source soaked my feet. My ankles. My thighs.

The dark painter continued to cover the box. The water rose. My chest tightened. My eyes became wild and my hair hung around my shoulders. I pounded on the box with the palms of my hands.

"Please don't paint the Haint Blue, don't paint the Haint Blue," I yelled.

Blue paint covered the last spot on my glass coffin. Water rushed over my body. I pressed my mouth against the glass searching for pockets of air. Ears filled with water. Mouth filled with water. Nose filled with water. My eyes closed against the rush.

❁ ❁ ❁

I woke up gasping.

I shook myself awake and calmed my heart with the yoga *breath of life*. The recurring dreams were getting worse. What was going on with me, I wondered?

I jittered out of bed, made myself a cup of tea, and fired up the lap-top. Wrapped in my vintage wool blanket I took my breakfast of hot tea and kolache to the back deck. The rich smell of Earl Gray filled my nose as the hot liquid warmed my belly.

H-A-I-N-T (space) B-L-U-E I typed.

"Okay internet, whatcha got for me?"

Porch ceilings were more often than not painted blue in the South. Inhabitants continue to paint porch ceilings blue because that's what their grandfather did, and that's what his grandfather did.

Many Southerners advise that blue porch

ceilings originated from the fear of haints. Southerners have a special name for the ceiling paint used on porches — the soft blue-green is referred to as *Haint Blue*. Haints are restless spirits of the dead who, for whatever reason, have not moved on from their physical world.

Haint Blue, which can also be found on door and window frames as well as porch ceilings, is intended to protect the homeowner from being taken or influenced by haints. It is said to protect the house and the occupants of the house from evil.

It is also believed that blue paint repels insects, allowing a porch bug-free and pleasant during long summer afternoons and evenings.

There is some debate; most credible sources discredit this belief. However, this idea could be steeped in historical truths: when blue paints were first used on ceilings, they were most likely milk paints, which had lye mixed into the formula. Lye is a known insect repellent, which would explain why insects would avoid the painted ledge or porch ceiling. Many still hypothesize that insects prefer not to nest on blue ceilings because they are fooled into thinking the blue paint is actually the sky.

The phone rang and shattered my budding epiphany. I knew it had something to do with my dream and Haint Blue, but the thoughts were lost.

"Hello?"

Nothing. Static.

"Hello, is someone there?" Still nothing. I hung up.

I ran my fingers through my hair and stared across the yard. I remembered the strange foliage patterns I had seen from above.

I crunched across the leaf littered yard heading for the far corner. Weathered cement blocks poked out from their blanketed sleep. The hairs on the back of my neck pricked up. Another spider chill ran down my spine. I followed the old footings. A twig snapped behind me. My heart leaped into my mouth. I whirled around.

Nothing.

I couldn't shake the feeling of being followed. I picked up a fallen branch and used it as a broom to remove a carpet of leaves. Underneath was a bolted wooden shield. The hasp and hinges were old and rusted, but try as I might, I couldn't force any movement.

The phone rang and I sprinted for the porch.

"Hello," I panted into the receiver.

"Good morning Beautiful." He'd called me that since we started dating. I smiled, ached and realized I missed him more than I thought.

"Good morning Handsome," I replied trying to catch my breath.

"You sound like you've just run a marathon."

"No, just running from the back yard. I found a really weird wood thing in the ground. I think it could be a door to an old root cellar maybe or maybe a tornado shelter?"

"I told you there's no tornados in this part of Texas," he chuckled. "No, no, it's a well."

"A well? Hmm. Think we could tap it for watering the garden?"

"I don't think so. Kristine said the previous owners had it tested and it's no good. The water's got something wrong with it. They had it tested and then re-sealed when they bought the house fifty years ago."

"Maybe we should get it re-tested? Fifty years is a long time. Hey what are you doing calling me so early? No sleeping in?"

"Not if I want anything good for breakfast. Yesterday I slept in and there was nothing left but bruised bananas. Plus all the bigwigs are down there in the morning. Good for networking. I hope this job is just a stepping stone, you know? So, how goes things with the house? Getting your kitchen unpacked?"

"Miss my cooking, do ya?" I said with a proud smile.

"Always. This training is good, but too long. I think they could have condensed it into three days instead."

"Well, at least you're getting paid for it."

"True."

"Hey, speaking of money, I was thinking of buying some

paint."

"Well you know I don't care what you buy, but I wanna pick out paint colors too."

"Yeah, I just—want to paint the porch ceiling—blue." He tried to cut me off but I rushed on. "Before you say no, I know it doesn't go with our color scheme, but Kristine was telling me about *Haint Blue* keeping away hornets and evil spirits. It's a very traditional southern thing to do. I looked it up on the internet. Check it out, I sent you a link."

"Okay Babe, well, you know I'm a sucker for historical stuff. I'll check it out, but can't you wait 'till I get back?"

"Yeah, I guess. I just feel weird in this big old house by myself. I really miss you and the kids."

"What? Are you afraid we have ghosts and you can protect yourself with blue paint?"

I hesitated. I wanted to say yes, or maybe, but neither of us really believed in that stuff.

"No, I don't know. I guess I'm just anxious to have you home."

"I'll be home soon. Hey, I gotta run, Babe. Love ya"

"Love you too."

※ ※ ※

"Hi, I'm here to see Mr. Neiderlind," I said to the chubby girl behind the desk.

"He's over in the activity room." She gestured with her head, not glancing up from her phone.

"Um, I'm sorry, I've not met him before. Could you point him out?"

"Oooh, okay. We get lots like you. He's our town's living historian. You can't miss him. He always wears a black and white jacket and a funny hat," she said, her fingers not missing a beat in her text messaging, not once making eye-contact with me.

I found him just like she said. He looked like a grape that had been left in the back of the fruit drawer. His tiny head sat beneath a red fez. A houndstooth jacket encased his shrunken frame.

"Hello Mr. Neiderlind, my name is Helen. I'm a friend of Kristine Carter. She thought you might be able to tell me a little history on my house."

"Ja, she did, did she? Vhat a pretty thing you are. You know you remind me of my Rose. Sit, sit."

His thick German accent surprised me.

"She was my second wife. I've buried four. So, no more for old Gunther Neiderlind. Ah, but then, for you, I might make an exception."

He patted my hand and innocently flirted. I smiled and blushed. It had been a while since anyone bothered to flirt with me.

"So vhat haus have you gotten yourself?"

"Oh, we're the big cream colored house over on Crest, between Live Oak and Pecan."

His face turned dark.

"Oh that haus. Ahhh, I remember her."

"I'm sorry, her?"

"Ah never you mind, Vhat, vhat do you vant to know? It was built in 1907 by Germans my father knew. I helped paint it, you know. It was originally a dark green, green like magnolia leaves."

"Oh how lovely. We were going to go with green."

"I'm sorry, but I cannot remember the man's name. He built two houses with the same style. One of wood and one of brick. Maybe you ask them. It's two blocks away on Cedar, same haus numbers."

"Well actually, I was wondering...what I was wondering...." I sputtered and felt a bit sheepish. How could I bring death into the conversation with a man who looked like he had an appointment with the Grim Reaper this afternoon? "Has, has anything — tragic happened at my house?"

"Ahhh now we have it. You do want to know about her."

"I'm sorry. I still don't get what you mean."

"Vhat I mean. Vhat I mean. We were all in love mit her. She was the beauty of the town. As soon as the haus was done, she and her father moved in and enchanted us all. Every available man, and some unavailable," he winked, "wanted her. I was only twelve years old, but I, I wanted to run away mit her. She wasn't even that much older than me, maybe seventeen, eighteen, but she was engaged to that oil man. He was a mean one. Drank a lot. You know back then the square was full of saloons. Eh, he was rich.

Her father thought it was a good match. She didn't want to marry him."

"What makes you say that?"

"Well, she told me. I hung around you know, doing jobs for her father. I helped dig the well, too."

"Oh yes, it's still there, covered up though."

"Hmmmmm, is it still? Ja, her father and the oil man covered it before we finished it. They said the water vas no good. But, this was after." He lapsed into silence, then continued. "The house stood empty for years. No one wanted to buy it. It took a long time to change hands."

"I'm sorry. I think I missed something. After what?"

"After she disappeared, the oil man disappeared too. Nobody knows vhat happened and the father left not two weeks after. I think she ran away." His eyes clouded.

"Why, why would she do that?"

"Never mind, I'm tired now. These are bad memories you look for. Maybe she told him, maybe she didn't."

"Told him what?"

"That she loved another."

"Who?" You, I wanted to ask, but didn't have the guts.

"I know vhat you're thinking. I can see it in your pretty eyes. No, no, not me. I wish. I was just a kid to her. No, she'd fallen in love with my older brother, Heinrich." Pain and sorrow scored his face, tears trickled into deep crevices.

"Oh, I'm so sorry. I didn't mean to — I, I'll leave you alone.

I'm sorry. Thank you." I stood up and turned to go, but twisted back. "I'm sorry, just one more thing, what...what did she look like?"

His face relaxed into a smile that glowed like morning sun.

"She had skin like a porcelain doll, golden honey colored hair, and green-blue eyes."

A chill streamed across my body as I hurried out of the nursing home. My head ached and whirled; I rubbed my forehead for relief and found none. Goose pimples erupted on my arms, my efforts to rub them down failed. Outside, dark skies loomed overhead, the wind had picked up and dead leaves whispered across the pavement. The breeze was cool and damp. A storm was on its way.

❧ ❧ ❧

He had hold of her hair. Golden ribbons tumbled down from their pinned place.

"Who do you think you are?" he yelled and slapped her across the face. She gave a sharp cry but stifled the pain.

"I know who I'm not. I'm not you're wife." She stared at him defiantly.

"Not yet, you ungrateful bitch. But when I'm finished with you, no one else will have you."

He reached for the poufy sleeve of her dress. She tugged away and the sleeve ripped from the bodice. The pale skin of her exposed shoulder glowed in the moonlight. Her long dress swished and slowed her run. He bounded after her, lunged and tackled her to the ground.

Her head hit first. A sickening thwack echoed in the air as it connected with the bricks on the unfinished well.

The world tilted and I was no longer an observer, my consciousness shifted into her body. A rush of pain entered me. Worldly sounds were muffled. My head throbbed. My body was tugged and rolled. Then I fell, endlessly plummeting into squelchy dark. Dank earthy smells filled my nose. I reached up and touched the back of my bloody head. A cry escaped my lungs before the cold water enveloped me.

I woke up screaming.

"What? What is it?" My husband groped for the light. The stark white light burned my eyes before they adjusted.

"Just another dream," I said.

"Honey, this is getting ridiculous. You've woken up every night with some kind of nightmare. You're really worrying me and you've never screamed before."

"This time it was different. This time I know what needs to be done."

"Good, does that mean we can go back to sleep," he said with a yawn, "no more nightmares?"

"Do you trust me?"

"Always."

"Okay, go back to sleep, but we're calling the Sheriff in the morning, and we're opening that well."

"Okay, crazy baby."

I playfully bonked him on the head with my pillow as he sank back into sleep. I rose to start a very long day.

Elsa Gertrude Klein. That was her name.

The Live Oak rustled and sang a gentle song as I leaned down and placed lilies on the fresh grave. An ache opened up in my chest and my eyes bristled with tears. I didn't know why. I didn't know her in life but couldn't help feeling like I did. Sorrow and loss consumed me. I would miss her and knew I would have no more dreams. But just in case, we'd settled on a blue, *Haint Blue*, and right after Christmas we'd paint the porch ceiling.

It had taken longer than I thought it would to get her a proper resting place. I knew she was down there, but the Sheriff thought we were nutters. I hired Bubba, the guy who kept coming round asking us if we had any odd jobs for him. Well, I had an odd job all right. Bubba got into climbing gear and went down in the well and dug for me. When he came back up with bones, the Sheriff finally called in a team.

What's funny about *Mayberry* is everyone has grown up together or is related to one another. So if you want something done, like say forensics on hundred year old bones, you just call your cousin. I didn't need a coroner to tell me who she was and how she died. Plus there was the locket, with the initials EGK, tangled around her bony ribcage.

I went to see Neiderlind, and he confirmed her name. I feared he would have a heart attack, but he wept and put up the money for her headstone and buried her next to his brother. I let Neiderlind keep the locket.

As I stood from the Elsa's grave a wave of dizziness threatened to topple me, my vision tunneled. I leaned against the great oak and squeezed the back of my neck until the vertigo passed, but my head throbbed. I pulled out my phone.

"Hey Handsome."

"Hey Beautiful, how'd it go?"

"Fine. I'm glad it's over. You on the square with the kids?" I massaged my neck.

"Yeah, are you on your way over? I think it really is *Mayberry* or the closest thing you can come to it in this age. You've got to see these characters dressed up in their costumes. And just to warn you, the kids want costumes for next year." He chuckled.

I tugged at my ear as my headache spread to that side.

"Listen, I've got a really bad headache. I'm gonna run home, take some Motrin and rest. I'll meet you guys in a couple hours?"

He grumbled. "Well, okay, just don't miss the parade and the lighting of the Yule Log."

"I promise, I'll be there."

* * *

The rich smell of Earl Gray filled my nose as the hot liquid warmed my belly. I nibbled on a kolache. We sat on the wide beautiful porch in handsome wicker chairs.

"It's my favorite, too," she said.

Her honey hair was swept up into a graceful pile on top her head, dainty earrings dangled from her ears. Delicate lace ruffled around her neck, her full skirt fanned across the chair. She reached across the table and squeezed my hand.

"I can't thank you enough. I'm sorry if I frightened you. I didn't mean to."

"I know you didn't." I marveled at how young she was. How beautiful. My heart ached and my eyes filled with tears.

"Please don't cry. I won't bother you again. It was hard to communicate between worlds and I never wanted you to feel my pain." She rose and sat next to me. "I have a gift for you."

She gently pressed her cool lips to my forehead. Smells of summertime and orange blossoms filled the air.

I woke up laughing.

The twilight cast impossible shadows on the small town. Christmas carolers crooned in the distance. I made my way to the square. Everything was glowing. Everyone was glowing. Everywhere I looked I saw living auras pulse and shine. Blues, greens, yellows, violets, and reds wreathed bodies like giant halos. My heart swelled and my insides fluttered. My Harvey glowed gorgeous greens, his kindness glimmering in the night air. My children shone like stars, their light filled with purity. I looked down and saw my own warm aura, fervid in the darkness and tilted my head toward the heavens. What a gift.

"Merry Christmas, Elsa."

11. ZELDA

elda tottered into her room and plopped onto the velvet vanity chair. Her gossamer dress floated like a cloud and settled around her thighs and knees. Iridescent sequins winked as the maid, Lexi, leaned down to unbutton Zelda's shoes. Lexi slipped Zelda's feet out of the delicate slippers and returned the footwear to their resting place among the other hundred shoes in Zelda's closet.

"It was a lovely party, wasn't it Lexi?"

"Yes ma'am." Lexi answered, her Scottish accent thick with the late hour. "Let's get you into bed, ma'am."

"Lexi, you know I hate to be called ma'am or Madame. Call me Miss. Now, did you see me dancing with the young men?" She sighed. "I miss Glenn. I miss Karl. Did you ever meet Karl before the...." She left the sentence unfinished.

"No ma'am, I mean Miss. But your cousin, Mr. Glenn, he

was a bonny lad. We haven't seen him since Mr. Karl was...."

"A horrible tragedy. I—don't want to talk about his death." She sat up, and for a minute, livened, then sank back into her malaise. "Where has all the fun gone, Lexi?" She unclipped her diamond earrings and tossed them onto the vanity. "Who did Mr. Worthington dance with tonight? I lost track of him."

"Couldn't say, Miss, but there were none as lovely as you and you kept right up with those new Charleston steps."

"Yes I did, didn't I?"

Lexi helped Zelda undress, then guided her pyjama top over her head. Zelda stepped out of her rolled stockings and into the wide leg pyjama bottoms that swished like tide pools around her ankles. Lexi pulled back the crisp sheets and Zelda climbed in.

"Good night Mrs. Worthington," Lexi said and turned the light off. The door clicked softly behind her.

Zelda pulled the eye mask over her eyes and settled her golden head on her pillow. She didn't think Bart would come tonight. She wasn't sure if she was relieved or saddened. She was more apathetic than anything, and indifferent to her apathy. She couldn't remember the last time she really felt anything. She could, but she had locked it away and refused to remember it.

She didn't hear the door, but was surprisingly pleased when the space next to her sank with her husband's weight. She reached out to touch him, but no one was there. Disconcerted by her deceived perception, she bolted upright and switched on the light. She was alone.

It must have been dreams and reality blending before sleep, she reasoned to herself. She punched her pillow into a comfortable ball, turned off the light and lay back down. The mattress sagged again and this time she felt the distinct pressure of someone's head on the pillow next to hers.

Her haze and lassitude evaporated as she scrambled out of bed. Her heart pounded in her ears. She fell to the floor with a thump, caught in the covers. Harsh laughter echoed in the room. When she turned on the light, the cackle stopped. Her heart raced faster and a thin sheen of sweat covered her lithe body. The curtains swayed. Her head jerked toward the movement.

"Is someone there?" She called and stood up. It could have been a drunken party goer. It had happened before, though not in her room, not on this floor. But inebriated guests, or those looking for privacy, often ended up in the oddest places in the large house.

"Who's there," she asked again and moved toward the windows. This time her eyes whipped back to her dressing table. She thought she caught movement in the mirror, then realized it must be her own reflection. Thinking herself silly she made an effort to calm down.

Then a force crashed into her; though not strong, it caught her off guard and she lost her balance. Her hands flailed, grasping at air as she toppled onto the plush carpet. A cackle of laughter crowed from every corner. She had the sensation of being draped in cobwebs, and she beat and slapped at the invisible veil. She felt like she was losing her mind and thought if anyone was watching, it would look like it, too.

Suddenly, the images she had tucked so carefully away forced their way to the surface. She remembered that night...

※ ※ ※

Karl had wanted her to leave Bart, and had wanted her to announce it at the dinner they'd planned at the house. She loved Karl, but a part of her loved Bart, too, or loved the security and title that came with the Bartholomew Worthington name. She wasn't sure. She wasn't sure it mattered. But the vibrant feeling that Karl had re-awakened was beginning to fade, and she wondered if it would always be that way. She didn't consciously question it, but a spark of doubt tainted her ideal of Karl and the life he had in mind for her. Would it be so different than her life with Bart? She was confused, so she drank. But she always drank. She didn't want to choose. Why couldn't they all continue the way they were...pretending.

On the way back from the city, Zelda had insisted on driving Karl's Gold Bug Speedster, though she wasn't much practiced at it. The top was down, and the wind blew fresh on her face. Her skin tingled with possibilities. All doubt fled her mind as Karl squeezed in tight beside her, his foppish hair dancing on her cheek. The lights of the city ebbed and became a backdrop of stars as they drove across the train track.

The headlamps illuminated a figure in front of them. Karl cranked the steering wheel, but not quickly enough. Green eyes stared into Zelda's with a look of shock before the face that belonged to them slammed into the windshield and cracked the glass. The body bounced and rolled to the side as the car skidded to a stop. Zelda bit her lip so hard she drew blood.

Karl traded places with her, took the steering wheel and peeled away just as people came out of the gas station diner. Zelda couldn't stop herself from looking back. Brassy red hair circled a once pretty face; blood ran into the unblinking eyes. A man fell to his knees at the body, but Zelda could still see the eyes, and she thought they looked into hers with acute accusation.

After a few moments, the memory faded, but her ragged breath caught in her throat and she hiccupped in a most unladylike way. She reached for the edge of the bed-covers, dragged them over her head and tucked them around her body, drawing herself into a ball. She told herself lie after lie until all traces of that night and the evening's delirium vanished.

Mabel

Mabel understood why Barty had sought her out. She was everything his wife wasn't. Where Zelda was pale and lithe, Mabel had freckles and rosy skin. Barty would kiss every tan freckle while his hands massaged her ample breasts and hips. Zelda didn't have those either — she had the thin boyish body of the ladies in magazine ads.

And Zelda was as much fun as a turnip in bed. Mabel had seen them, spied on them. Mabel was fun in bed. She laughed in bed. She did everything Barty asked her to do and liked it, never ashamed or embarrassed. Nothing felt dirty or wrong. But after seeing that he still screwed his wife too, she felt used and betrayed. Mabel followed him into the city and found him with another mistress, a brunette this time.

Mabel had never thought of herself as a mistress. She was his girlfriend, and future wife. He'd bought her bright dresses with fringe, beaded high heels and an ermine cape. They'd spent hours with her friends in motel rooms, gin joints, and speak-easies. He'd liked to watch her dance in the dim smoky light of the underground clubs. Surely he'd felt more than lust for her.

After the accident, Mabel hung around the gas station. Even though she had no love or sympathy for the husband she'd intended to leave, she had nowhere else to go. Barty hadn't been seen for almost a year. She'd heard they were out of the country.

Finally, Barty's shiny Pierce Arrow stopped for gasoline. The cream paint gleamed like the sun. Neither Barty nor Stanley, her hapless husband, noticed when she slipped into Barty's car. He took her away from the gas station to the big mansion. She'd dreamt about living there and now thought she could.

It didn't work. She finally understood she would never belong in the big house, and Barty never had any intention of marrying her. She followed him around and taunted him, trying to get him to notice her. But he would never see her. She was nothing to him. She finally understood. She was something he once owned and had grown bored of, like last year's tie. He would never be affected by her.

He treated his wife the same way, but that didn't make Mabel hate her any less. Zelda. Now, Zelda was someone Mabel might be able to affect or, hopefully, destroy.

Zelda

It'd been days since Zelda's hallucination. She didn't tell anyone. She thought about telling Lexi, but wasn't sure she could trust her. She wasn't sure she could trust anyone. She could've trusted Glenn. He hadn't wanted anything from her and loved her like only a cousin could, no expectations, no competition, no desire. She had trusted Glenn, but after the funeral he'd disappeared. She'd heard he was writing a book. She wondered if she'd gone to Karl's funeral, if Glenn would've forgiven her, not that there was anything to forgive, but maybe he would've stayed.

Still feeling a little unbalanced, she went to her bathroom to retrieve the Lithium prescribed to her after the accident. The room was unusually cold, her skin prickled and she wondered if she was coming down with a summer cold. That would explain a lot, she reasoned. She opened the medicine cabinet. Maggots crawled over her bottles, tubes, and containers, tiny wiggling, squirming white worms.

She slammed it shut and shook her head. She was imagining things again. She pulled the embroidered hand towel from its ornate ring and dabbed her neck and temples with cold water. Her pale face revealed the very beginnings of age, her beauty dimming. She stretched her neck and turned her head, touching her chin where the skin wasn't as taut as it used to be. A face with red hair and green eyes peered at her from behind her shoulder. She recognized the face, those eyes. Mabel. She jumped and spun, bruising her hip on the sink. No one was there.

Then she heard the faint squeak of the door handle, slowly twisting.

"Lexi, is that you?" she called in a meek voice. "Bartholomew? Jasper? Who's there?"

The door began to shake, wood banged against wood and metal clanged against metal, reminding her of squealing brakes. Her heart jumped into her throat and her mouth filled with saliva. Her hands began to quake, then her arms, then her torso, and then her entire body. She thought she might be sick.

Then it stopped. Only she couldn't stop shaking. She reached for the handle, afraid it would burn or shock her, but it turned easily beneath her trembling hand. She climbed into bed without changing out of her two-piece nautical ensemble and rang for Lexi. Even though Zelda had seen the bottle of lithium crawling with maggots, Lexi couldn't find it, nor any sign of bugs. She brought Zelda hot tea and called the doctor. Zelda emptied the contents of her whiskey bottle into the porcelain teapot when no one was looking.

Mabel

After weeks of toying with Zelda, Mabel was delighted. A few more tricks and she'd have her in a strait jacket or jumping off the balcony. Is that what she wanted? She asked herself. What did she want? She wanted justice. She wanted Zelda to pay for hitting her. Killing her. Murdering her with Karl's car.

Zelda

Bartholomew and the doctor spoke in hushed tones that matched the twilight hue of the bedroom. Zelda couldn't hear what they were saying, which only increased her agitation. She couldn't sleep, but couldn't get out of bed, either. The doctor had said something about a nervous crisis. She knew she was having a crisis but couldn't tell Bart she was being haunted by a red-haired hussy. That would be admitting too much, too many truths.

But maybe she could tell him about the accident; about how she drove and not Karl, and Mabel's husband had shot the wrong man. But if Mabel's husband hadn't shot Karl, then...but it didn't matter. All that mattered was for her to confess. But Karl hadn't been screwing Mabel, and who told Mabel's husband Karl was the one driving?

"Bart," she yelled to her husband. He shook the doctor's hand as Lexi saw him out.

"What is it dear?"

"Bart, I have to tell you something."

He sat on the edge of her bed. "I really don't have time, darling. I need to be at the golf course in ten minutes. Can't it wait?" He patted her hand.

"I—I'm, I'm the one who ran over the girl, that woman with the red hair."

"Oh, is that what this is about. I know that darling. You think I don't know Karl was protecting you?" Too many truths. She didn't want to talk about it, but he continued. "You were quite foolish, but you're done with that aren't you?"

"Yes, yes," she shook and squeezed the last tears from her eyes. "But should I confess it to the police?"

"Ah well, if it will make you feel better, but I've got the best lawyers in the city and there isn't a judge or jury who would convict you."

"Oh." She wiped her eyes and blew her perfect nose.

"All better now. Get some rest. I'll check on you when I get back." He leaned in to kiss her, then shifted uncomfortably, reached over and patted her bottom.

Mabel

Mabel witnessed the breakdown, but it didn't turn out the way she thought it would. She had not broken Zelda and didn't understand how the woman could live with herself.

What was wrong with the world? Suddenly, a force pulled at her like yarn unraveling from a sweater. Her mind grappled at threads.

Were there varying degrees of justice? Was *she* unjust in her haunting? She wondered if justice existed at all. Her thoughts spun away and were diminished until there was nothing left. She became as hollow as the people she had sought to be.

12. MRS. FRANKLIN'S NIGHT OUT

hunder shakes the house and lightning strobes her eyes, the lights flicker. Not now, not tonight, she thinks. I need this. I need just one night of not being a slave to two little children, of not being a lonely housewife of a sailor who is never home. I've done my duty and taken them trick-or-treating. The children are happy in their sugar comas and a sitter is on the way. She knows she is blessed with healthy children, a roof over her head, food in the cupboard and a faithful husband. Somehow it's not enough. It should be, but it isn't. She misses him. She misses dancing. She misses dancing with him.

Mrs. Franklin dusts gold powder onto her naked eye lid. Lightning flashes again, thunder booms. Maybe I should stay home? No. No I can't. I won't. She pictures women in beautiful gowns, pin-curled hair, dangling jewels. Handsome men in suits and hats, festooning an Art Deco ballroom, masqued — all masqued. I've always wanted to go to a masquerade dance. Lightning and thunder crack simultaneously. So close, so close. It rattles her nerves and shakes her resolve.

For weeks she's sewn and embroidered a full-length satin gown with vintage beaded trim. She aches for an evening of beauty and prays it will resemble a Jane Austen ball from her favorite novels. She often sets herself up for disappointment, but hasn't found a way to taper her puerile optimism. And now fate has conspired against her. Her best friend and adventurous cohort is stuck at work. She finds it passing strange that no one else from the Historic Society received invitations or had ever heard of the event, but she is determined to go...even if it is alone.

Sitter in place, Mrs. Franklin makes her escape into the dank ragged night. Rain streams down the car window. Lightning illuminates the dark avenue in time to see a black cat dart in front of her car. She swerves and saves its life, looks up and finds a shadowy mass in front of her. Oncoming headlights blind her eyes. Sweaty hands slide on the steering wheel, delaying reactions. Her mouth tastes of tin. Flickered light illuminates the vehicle's occupants. Wipers swipe and momentarily clear the view. Confusion and panic distort their faces. Tires slide and glide. The world sways. Lightning and thunder collide with a crash of sight and sound.

The rain subsides. Dark clouds swallow the moon and lend the street a pale gray pallette. Her heels tick-tock as she approaches the hulking edifice, street lamps contract in its looming presence. She pulls her faux fur cape tighter and shivers. Her thinning strands of beauty cling to her like wet tissue paper.

What am I doing here alone? What if Miss Parker can't meet me here at all? Maybe I should go back. Maybe I should have waited to see when she could get off work. Maybe I should have listened to my mother, *married women have no business going out dancing without their husbands*. Maybe I have the wrong address?

She pulls the vellum invitation from her handbag. Thin calligraphy lines confirm the location. A cold breeze snatches the invitation, tumbling it down the deserted sidewalk. A scrawny black cat pounces on it and chases it down the block.

"Go back, go back go, back," it mews.

She shakes her head laughing at how an anxious mind can turn a cat's cry into intelligible words.

"Poor little thing," she says aloud, skittering after the cat.

Her feet slide on the slick sidewalk. She grabs the brass door handles to keep from falling, steadies herself, and lets her fingers linger on the cool metal etching of the ornate doors. Fingertips trace the intricate sunbeam pattern emanating from a gilded shield. How beautiful, how elegant, she thinks. The cat out of sight and misgivings forgotten, she pushes the doors open.

Glamour and style beguile her eyes. Swirling, curling brass railings line the stairway to the balcony where dapper men bound up and down. Pretty shoes peek through the balustrade of the mezzanine. A massive crystal chandelier hangs from a gold-leaf sky. Cloth covered tables perch like white vultures on the edge of the dance floor. Her hair combs—which will later be lost and swept away—glint in the luminous light.

I wish my Mr. Franklin could be here. She feels naked without her husband, like a skirt caught in underwear. It is an uncomfortable feeling to which she is accustomed, only in quiet moments of longing does she feel the breeze of this exposure.

She selects a table that allows her a view of the front door and the stage.

"What can I get for you Mrs. Franklin?"

Mouth agape, she is confused at how he should know her name and embarrassed to be caught sitting alone.

"Oh, I will take a glass of champagne please," she answers, rattled.

The half-masqued waiters are costumed too, covered eyes with long protruding noses, disconcerting and sinister, but delightful in every detail. She loves themes and the promoters have certainly outdone themselves recreating a Mozartian masquerade. She sips her champagne. Sweet berry notes flavor the citrus edge, effervescence tingles her tongue. It's been too long since she's been kissed.

Mr. Maxwell DeMille, the emcee, takes the stage in an impeccable tuxedo and pencil thin mustache, looking like a man dipped in wax. He introduces the musicians with his scratchy vintage voice. The conductor taps the podium and orchestral sounds saturate the room.

She glances toward the entrance, hoping to see her friend, when a shadow falls across the door and sends a shiver up her spine. She shudders and remembers what her mother used to say: *Whenever you get a chill it means a goose is walking over your grave.*

The dance floor is crowded but not unmanageable. Glorious gowns glide across the floor laid out in minuets and waltzes. Mrs. Franklin aches to dance, feels the singularity of her unaccompanied position and decides it's time to look around for a gentleman suitor.

Leaning against a large wooden pillar stands a trim man with slick dark hair, his coif creased where the masque is tied to his head. Something about the way he stands reminds her of her husband. A laugh from a swirling coryphée steals her attention. When she looks back the man is gone.

She takes another sip of champagne and traces the ring on her third finger. It sparkles and winks back the memory of the day Mr. Franklin placed it there.

*   *   *

She'd gone to see him graduate from Boot Camp. The day was brisk and gray and they found refuge in the quaint Pasta Fina Ristorante. When alone, amidst the old photographs, the spicy aromas, the wafting WWII music and the delicate table settings, he fumbled his words, explaining that he hadn't planned on asking her to marry him today. He wanted to plan better, but she looked so beautiful and he was so stunned that she had traveled all this way to see him, and something about this place, this time, this setting—felt right. Would she do him the honor of being his wife?

The antique ring, his grandmother's, that he'd procured just weeks before, glistened in its satin bed.

"Yes, yes a thousand times yes," she'd said as he slid it on her left hand, third finger.

※ ※ ※

She looks up to find the handsome stranger in front of her, hand outstretched.

"May I have this dance?" he asks. His silken voice slides down her skin and tickles her breasts.

"I would be honored," she rejoins.

He smells of expensive cologne and something else, something old, something wet. It must be the musky scent of damp wool she decides. What he leads she does not recognize, but follows without effort. He swirls her into a maelstrom of spins and steps until the final crescendo of the song comes to a juddering halt. Dipped in a low repose, she opens eyes she didn't know were closed. Not releasing her from this horizontal embrace, he whispers deliciously into her ear.

"You know if we were in Europe we would dance another."

"Oh, then let's pretend we're in Europe," she purrs.

Despite the bite of new heels, and the unease of not

knowing a soul, she relishes the satin sliding across her hips, winding and unwinding with each twist and turn on the dance floor. She feels like a princess or a heroine, something lovely from a story book.

"Do you live here?" he inquires.

"No. Yes. No, not in this old part of town, I drove down from the North."

"Are you staying somewhere nearby?" he asks, hopeful.

"No, I must drive back tonight."

"Perhaps."

He winks and kisses her hand, steering her back to her seat. She takes too big a draught of champagne and the bubbles prick her nose and water her eyes. She dabs at them with the starched linen napkin. It scrapes across her delicate skin.

"If you'll excuse me, I need to visit the lounge." She coughs into her napkin.

"But of course," he replies.

Folding her napkin, she drapes it across the back of the chair and makes her way toward the ladies lavatory. Her drop earrings jingle as she ascends the mahogany staircase. Gaining the height of the second floor she surveys the room with a satisfied smile. She would never cheat on her husband but hasn't felt this alive in years. Blooming with the attention and revelry, she is happy to play the coquette for a night.

The hand-painted door shuts behind her, squelching all sound. The powder room is deathly quiet, save for the rhythmic drip of a leaky faucet. She sits at the vanity and pulls the powder case from her purse and dusts her nose. From the row of stalls behind her, a slithering noise, as if something wet is being dragged across clotted mud, startles her. Slither, rasp, scrape. A shiver washes across her body. Slither, rasp, scrape. Loose powder tumbles from her compact and sprinkles the countertop. Slither, rasp, scrape. She rests her shaking hands in her lap.

"Hello," she calls out, "hello."

Nothing.

She returns to the mirror. Slither, rasp, scrape. A dark shadow teases the edge of the oval frame. Slither, rasp, scrape. She trembles, teetering on her chair. Her heart beats faster. Slither, rasp, scrape. She inches her head around and holds her breath not sure what she expects to see. Slither, rasp, scrape.

"Hello!" she cries out again. "Is anyone there?"

She springs to her feet peering into the narrow hall of stalls. Slither, rasp, scrape. Her breath forms a soft cloud in front of her lips, the room unexpectedly cold. Slither, rasp, scrape. Sucking wet sounds lap at her ears. Slither, rasp, scrape. Slither, rasp, scrape. Breathing loud and ragged, she gulps air and holds it tight. What is that noise?

Squeeeeeeak. The door swivels open. A young woman steps from the furthest stall, her dress an exquisite historic reproduction in soft rose satin. Mrs. Franklin exhales noisily.

"Begging your pardon Miss. I didn't mean to startle you," the young woman says with a slight brogue.

"Didn't you hear me call hello?" Mrs. Franklin asks.

"No I'm sorry, Miss, tis deadly quiet in the wee back corner."

"Well I...well I. I'm sorry I didn't mean to sound harsh. It's just that I thought I was alone. I am alone. I mean my friend...could not...it's late is all."

"No, no, not alone as it turns out." The young woman adjusts her masque tightening the satin ties.

"Oh, here, let me help you with that." Mrs. Franklin reaches for her.

"No," the girl refuses, pulling away. "No thank you. You best be putting your masque back on. There is no taking 'em off until the witching hour."

"The witching hour?"

"Uh...midnight, you know, like the New Year when everything changes over. Then all is unmasked."

"Yes, I recall something about that in the invitation." She shakes her head. "Your dress is lovely."

"Thank you kindly, Miss. So's yours."

Mrs. Franklin smiles and turns to the mirror admiring her hand-made gown. The young girl cracks the door to leave. Light slashes across her costume and coif coloring the girl's raven hair — gray?

"Wait!" calls Mrs. Franklin, but the girl is gone.

Silence cloaks the room, not even the drip of the faucet echoes. She gathers her compact, applies fresh lipstick and tidies the counter. Sliding her masque into place, she steadies herself to brave the ballroom alone.

She wishes she would have asked the young woman to have a drink with her. She wishes Miss Parker would show. Their friendship bloomed after admiring each other's vintage attire in the commissary.

Discovering that her husband and Miss Parker's boyfriend were attached to the same ship was a bonus. Joining the Historic Society together was a distraction from their loneliness.

Upon her return, she is surprised to find her roost crowded with colorful celebrants. A tableau of men in dazzling tuxedos and women in stunning gowns are crushed around the table. Their attire only surpassed by animal grotesqueries they wear over their faces: sinister cat visages with thin wire whiskers, haughty birds glittering with proud plumage and protuberant beaks. One woman's masque drips seabed pearls worthy of Amphitrite herself.

"I hope you don't mind darling. The place is absolutely packed with the dance floor being cleared," says the woman wearing an asymmetric jeweled masque. Her flinty gray eyes reveal no warmth.

"Why is the dance floor cleared?" rejoins Mrs. Franklin.

The woman's exposed cheek curls with a half-smile.

"The floor show is about to begin dear."

"Tonight we have a very special treat, or should I say Trick or Treat," announces the waxy emcee. "Luckily for you revelers,

All Hallows Eve has fallen on a Sunday this year, and as you regular patrons know, Sunday is our night here. So please, sit back and enjoy a devil of a show. Without further ado, I give you the Ghost Sprites."

Tiny masqued women in gossamer gowns patter across the stage and drape themselves like weeping willows. The orchestra strikes a chord and the Ghost Sprites fly, flutter and draggle from stage to dance floor. Notes vacillate between high eerie violins and deep bellowing bass. Drums reverberate and compete with Mrs. Franklin's own heartbeat. She feels compelled to take gasping breaths of air, her noisy exhales lost in the cacophony. The requiem reaches a climax as tall thin men clad in red devil costumes shadow the women. Blood-red silhouettes lift the sprites into a waltzing dance. Fiends tower over the nymphs skewing the observer's perspective. The room bobs and sways not unlike the deck of a squalled ship.

The revelers rise and join the dance. Mrs. Franklin throbs with loneliness. She attempts a path to the door but is hemmed by the crush of the crowd. There is no way forward — only back. She retreats to the grand staircase trying to gain the solace of the lounge. The notes ring discordant in her ears as her head swims making her dizzy and weak. Suddenly one of the red devils is at her elbow. She recognizes the smell of expensive cologne and wet wool.

"Hi ho, where are you trying to get to Mrs. Franklin?" Relief at his attention overrides the confusion at him knowing her name. She does not remember giving it.

"I don't know where I'm trying to go," she stammers.

"Please return to your table. I will be with you in a minute. Just let me change."

She obeys, and before she can comfortably seat herself, he reappears in his previous elegant garb.

The bell tolls twelve. Bong, bong, bong....

Slither, rasp, scrape. The masques melt from the reveler's faces. Slither, rasp, scrape. She gasps and rises from her seat stepping in front of the gentlemen to get a better look.

Slither, rasp, scrape. Once bright dresses are torn and stained. Matted, dull hair hangs in clumps of ill-formed sausages. Light glints off bare bone. Elbow joints with putrid clinging flesh waggle as the women spin, their faces sicken with wicked grins. Slither, rasp, scrape. Previously smooth skin is melty and patchy, a threadbare quilt of sinewy filaments stretch over skulls. Deep eye sockets hold gray eyes, all of them gray, or no eyes at all. The dirge staggers and crashes with barely a thread of melody. The beating drums thump louder and faster, slither, rasp, scrape, deeper and heavier. Slither, rasp, scrape. The ballroom becomes a whirling dervish of macabre figures. Slither, rasp, scrape. They dance on.

Her stomach clenches, her face feels hot and icy at the same time, her hands clammy. Her breath comes in short gasps. She cannot get enough air. She feels the prick of tears behind her eyes and lets them overspill pooling into the edge of her masque.

"You can take off your masque now," says the silken voice behind her.

Deft fingers pull the bow-ends as her masque drops to the floor. She takes a staccato breath, steels herself and turns in the direction of the voice. Her hand flies to her mouth. Her forehead wrinkles in confusion.

"Just the way I remembered," he says recalling his last living thought before his lungs filled with water.

"Mr. Franklin?" she croaks.

Water drips from his suit as he stretches out a sallow hand.

"Shall we dance?"

ACKNOWLEDGMENTS

A very special thanks to the Rix Sisters, Roxanne and Gretchen who hosted the Scare the Dicken's Out of Us Literary Contest which started me on the road to Ghostoria.

Lockhart Texas Writer's group: Janet Christian, Gretchen Rix, Wayne Wathers, and Phil McBride for the wonderful workshop critiques.

To my mom, Judy Anderson, for listening and giving unsolicited straight advice when I needed it. To my husband for letting me check out of the family for hours on end.

Thank you to Jennifer Heishman, Liza McCarthy, and Clara Peterson for letting me bounce story ideas off you. Suzanne Fulton and Gretchen Pearson for reading. And Sondra Schaible, Patricia Forest, Marci Froh, Pagan Jackson and Helen Francis for killer beta readings and editing advice.

My carpool kids: Clara and Charles Francis, Naia Fulton-Jones, Ella McCarthy, Olivia Ybarra and Kathryn Peterson, for letting me pick your young brains.

Karen Phillips, www.phillipscovers.com for an original cover. Kathy Anderson at Anderson Business Support Services, www.andersonbusinesssupportservices.com for her amazing web design and unwavering belief in my writing.

Tam Francis

Photo by Brian Tassie

ABOUT THE AUTHOR

Tam Francis has taught swing dancing with her husband for fifteen years and is an avid collector of vintage patterns, vintage clothing and antiques.

She has published two indie magazines: From the Ashes (Arts & Literature 1990-1994) and Swivel: Vintage Living (Swing dancing, vintage lifestyle culture 1994-2000).

Tam has been a poet (two-time, National Poetry Slam City Team Member , Scottsdale Center for the Arts Poetry Art Walk Featured Poet, and New Times Featured Poet), Visual Voices Featured Writer and short story wordsmith.

Now a blogger and novelist, she is currently working on her *Girl in the Jitterbug Dress* series. This is her first short story collection. For 1940's slang, music, fashion and history, check out her blog at: www.girlinthejitterbugdress.com.

She now lives with her family in Lockhart, Texas in a 1908 home, which may or may not be haunted.

If you enjoyed these stories please take a moment to write a review on your favorite online outlet.

Thank you for reading.

Made in the USA
Charleston, SC
26 January 2015